OLD TALES OF CHINA

A book to better
understanding of China's stage,
cinema, arts and crafts

Written by Li Nianpei
Illustrated by Pang Xiquan
Sun Yizeng
Li Binsheng

Graham Brash, Singapore

中國傳統故事
OLD TALES OF CHINA

Written by Li Nianpei
Illustrated by Pang Xiquan, Sun Yizeng
Li Binsheng

Published by
GRAHAM BRASH PTE. LTD.,
36-C, Prinsep Street,
Singapore 0718.

Printed in the Republic of Singapore by
Chong Moh Offset Printing Pte. Ltd.

ISBN 9971 947 34 X

PREFACE

Tourists during their visit to China will inevitably come into contact with the vast treasurehouse of Chinese legend and folklore. Many would like to know the stories behind the names they hear mentioned, and learn more about the people memorialized at temples, parks and historical sites, the characters presented by the classical theatre and the traditional themes reflected in works of art or even articles of daily use. A need has been felt for a collection of ancient tales in handy book form, for although some material is available, the articles are scattered in various publications. This book has been prepared to satisfy this need within modest limits.

To facilitate consulting, the titles are arranged alphabetically according to their romanized Chinese versions, which are given in brackets following their respective English titles, with the exception of episodes from the five famous classical novels, which are placed at the end. An index at the end lists the Chinese names and titles with their transliterations both in the new *pinyin* and the Wade-Giles' system of romanization. This is to make it possible for the reader, upon hearing a name mentioned in Chinese, to locate the relevant text himself without the help of an interpreter.

The writer wishes to take this opportunity of expressing his heartfelt indebtedness to Miss Bertha Sneck of the Foreign Languages Press, Beijing for going over the manuscripts and making them more readable. Otherwise, the general conception of the book, the selection of subjects and materials and the structure of each tale, with all their inadequacies, remain his own. His gratitude also extends to Mr. Lu Niangao of the China Travel and Tourism Press, without whose en-

1

couragement the writing of this booklet would never have been attempted.

Li Nianpei

CONTENTS

2

ASHMA

阿詩瑪 (Ashma)

In the Stone Forest in Lunan county, Yunnan province of SW China there is a rock called Ashma Rock by the local folks. When you cry out loudly "Ashma, I am here" in front of the rock, it will echo "I am here . . . ". Who is Ashma? Why a rock? Here is the story.

Ashma is the young heroine of a long narrative poem, which has been handed down orally for generations by the Sani people (a branch of the Yi national minority) in Yunnan. The poem sings of her indomitable character and tells the story of how she fought for freedom and happiness against oppression and forced marriage.

Born into a poor family living in High Ajdee, she grew up as fair as she was deft at work and clever in mind. In fact, she was so beautiful that young men all over the land wished to woo her.

One of her suitors was Ajii, wayward son of the big wicked landlord Rabubalor, who lived in Low Ajdee. The father asked Hajow, a local official, to exert his power to act as the go-between in asking for Ashma's hand for his son.

Ashma's parents did not want their dear daughter to get married so soon and leave them. Hajow wagged his tongue and convinced them that girls must marry at the right age. At the mention of Rabubalor's name, however, Ashma, who had just returned from shepherding, grew angry. She made it very clear that she would have nothing to do with the landlord, not to say marrying his son. She pointed out that clear water would not mix with foul and lambs would not lie with jackals.

But willy-nilly, Ashma was dragged away by Rabubalor's kinsmen, who had come on horseback with the officer Hajow and feasted in Ashma's house, pronouncing the marriage sealed. Before being taken away, Ashma asked her desolate parents to call Ahay back to come to her rescue.

Now Ahay was Ashma's elder brother who, a good hunter and shepherd, was well-built and had a heart of gold. At

2

this time he was far away from home roaming with his herd in search of water and fresh grass. He had a bad dream one night and rushed home to see how things were. When learning of his sister's plight, he set out immediately on a fleet mare with bow and arrows to find the kidnappers.

Meanwhile, in Rabubalor's house, Ashma's will remained firm in spite of promises of wealth, threats and cruel whippings. She was locked up in a dark dungeon, but her hopes were aroused when she heard Ahay calling her.

Ajii barred the iron gate to keep Ahay from entering and challenged him to various difficult contests. So Ahay, after a ride of three days and nights, had to spend another three days and nights in these contests, all of which he won.

Still barred from entering, he shot three arrows at the house, one of which struck the shrine, another the wall and the third the door. These augured ill for the family, for the arrows were said to have magic power and could only be plucked out by good people, but not wicked. Rabubalor tried all means but not even the effort of strong men and five buffaloes was of any avail. Finally he had to concede and promise to let brother and sister go if they would pluck out the arrows.

Out they came at a slight pull by Ashma's dainty hand.

The landlord did not give up so easily. He asked Ahay to stay the night before setting out with his sister the next morning. During the night, the wicked landlord set free three tigers into the tower where Ahay was staying. The next morning, to his dismay, he found all three tigers killed and duly skinned. He had to let them go.

The path led along a ravine and a high mountain lake. Rabubalor and his men breached the dam of the lake, releasing torrents of water into the ravine just when Ashma and Ahay were passing through. Ahay tried hard to help his sister, but after a long and desperate struggle, Ashma was carried away by a powerful whirlpool.

3

When the waters receded, Ashma appeared, transformed into a rock, as graceful and dauntless as when she was alive. There the brave and beautiful girl still stands, ready to echo your call.

XIANG YU THE CONQUEROR PARTS WITH HIS CONSORT

霸王別姬 *(Ba Wang Bie Ji)*

The events took place in the year 202 B.C. after the fall of the Qin dynasty, when Liu Bang and Xiang Yu, at the head of two opposing forces, were contending for control of the empire.

Liu appointed Han Xin commander of an expedition in a strategic offensive against Xiang Yu. Han spotted a mountain in favourable terrain for a large-scale ambush and ordered one of his generals to feign surrender to Xiang in order to induce him to march his troops into the trap.

The scheme worked. Xiang Yu, who gave himself the title of "Ba Wang" (Prince Conqueror) and who was more renowned for his courage and physical prowess than for his shrewdness, took the bait and ordered an onslaught. This he did against the advice of his followers and of his favourite consort Yu Ji (Lady Yu), who usually accompanied him on his campaigns.

The result was a debacle for Xiang Yu, who found himself with his remnant army tightly encircled at a place called Gaixia (in present-day Anhui province).

Furthermore, Han got people to sing the popular songs of Chu all around Xiang Yu's troops. Now Chu was the place where Xiang had risen to fame, and most of his soldiers came from there. Hearing these songs made them homesick and gave them the strong suspicion that their homeland had fallen to the enemy. By this ruse, Han succeeded in demoralizing the Chu soldiers.

Xiang Yu, too, felt that the game was as good as lost. Lady Yu tried to console him but failed to dispel his qualms. She asked him to sit down for dinner in the army tent while she performed a graceful and dexterous double-sword dance to distract him from his worries.

But the news became worse every minute, with Liu Bang's troops intensifying their attacks and Xiang's own men deserting to the enemy. The only way out was to break through the encirclement.

Xiang Yu had his black steed brought to him. Confiding his apprehensions to it, he bemoaned the miserable end in store for them. In an extemporaneous song he also expressed his worries to the steed for the safety of Lady Yu, who by now had dissolved in tears.

Lady Yu, for fear that she might prove a burden to her husband in the attempt to break through, ended her life with a sword.

Xiang Yu fought gallantly through the encirclement with some hundred of his faithful followers until he arrived at the Wujiang River with twenty-six men left, still pursued by the enemy. A boatman offered to ferry him across to the east side of the river. The mention of "east side" reminded him of his start with 8,000 men of that region; now with nearly all of them lost, he asked himself, how could he face the elders of his homeland?

Seeing no way out, he ended his own life by the side of the river. He was only thirty-one. Thus a great hero met with his tragic end and the country was soon once again unified under a single dynasty, that of the Han (206 B.C.-220 A.D.).

THE EIGHT IMMORTALS CROSS THE SEA

八仙過海 *(Ba Xian Guo Hai)*

Legends about the Eight Immortals started to circulate orally long ago among the people and were recorded in the works of writers of the Tang and later dynasties. But it was only after Wu Yuantai of the Ming dynasty wrote *The Emergence of the Eight Immortals and Their Travels to the East* that the Eight began to be clearly distinguished as follows.

1) **Tieguai Li** (also called **Li Tieguai**, meaning Li with the Iron Crutch) was a lay Taoist by the name of Li Xuan who received his Enlightenment from the Supreme Patriarch of Taoism himself. Once his soul left his body to travel abroad but had to enter the corpse of a starved beggar when he found his own body mistakenly burnt by his disciple. He then had an earthly form with unkempt hair, a dirty face, a bare abdomen and a crippled leg. He blew water on the beggar's bamboo cane, changing it into an iron crutch. Hence his popular name. He is also generally shown carrying a gourd said to contain magic medicines.

2) **Han Zhongli** (or **Zhongli Quan**) was given the first divine revelations by Li Tieguai and then went into the mountains to seek the Light. After his return to this world, he killed a fierce tiger with a flying scimitar and changed copper into gold to help the poor. In the end, he ascended to the upper realms of immortality with his brother. He is usually shown with a feather fan in a comfortable reclining posture.

3) **Zhang Guolao** was a hermit in the Zhongtiao Mountains for a long time. He is said to have already been several hundred years old in the reign of Empress Wu Zetian (690-705 A.D.). Summoned by the Empress, he feigned death by magic in order to avoid meeting her. Later people saw him in the mountains near Hengzhou. He used to travel on a white donkey which could cover thousands of leagues in a single day. When taking a rest, he would fold up the donkey as if it were made of paper and put it into his suitcase. Emperor Xuan Zong summoned him to the capital. He played tricks to amuse the Sovereign, who bestowed several honorary titles

9

on him. He is usually depicted riding backward on his donkey, that is, facing the tail of the beast.

4) **He Xiangu** was a Tang dynasty girl of Zengcheng, Guangdong province, living at a place called Yunmu Xi (Ravine of Mica). She was said to have become an immortal at the age of fourteen by taking mica powder. After that, she was so agile of body that she could float from one peak to another, collecting fruit from the mountains for her mother. Another source says that she was a woman Taoist of Yongzhou during the Song dynasty, famous for her fortune-telling.

5) **Lan Caihe,** according to some sources, was a hermaphrodite, usually dressed in blue tatters, with one foot bare and the other in a boot, wandering through the country, begging along the thoroughfares and singing drunkenly to the cadence of castanets. One day in an inn, music of flutes and mouth-organs was heard descending from the sky, Lan was suddenly wafted off into the air and vanished.

6) **Lü Dongbin** was a native of Shaanxi (some say, of Shanxi) province and lived during the Tang dynasty. After failing twice at the imperial examinations during the years 841-846 A.D., he led a vagrant life for years. At the age of sixty-four, he met Han Zhongli, who taught him the secrets of alchemy. Then he became a hermit in the Zhongnan Mountains to seek the Way of Immortality. Later, he roamed the empire and was said to have killed vicious dragons at Jianghuai, played tricks with cranes at Yueyang, and performed various other magic arts to rid the world of evils. He was given an official title by a Yuan emperor and came to be generally known as Lü Zu (Patriarch Lü). Taoists considered him to be one of the five supreme deities of the North.

7) **Han Xiangzi** is said to be a distant nephew of the great Tang writer-statesman Han Yu. Intelligent and unrestrained in nature, he managed, once in an early winter, to make rose-peonies blossom in a few days in different colours,

10

each blossom carrying a written poem, to the great astonishment of his uncle. He tried to proselyte Han Yu to renounce his worldly affairs for Taoism. When Yu fell into disfavour and was banished to Chaoyang in the far south, he met with a heavy fall of snow on the way. Suddenly Xiangzi came from nowhere to bid him farewell. Before parting, Xiangzi told about future happenings, all of which came true.

8) **Cao Guojiu** is said to have lived during the Song dynasty and his name was Cao You, Guojiu being a semi-official title for the brothers of the empress. He had a brother who, taking advantage of his imperial connexion, became a notorious evil-doer. Ashamed of his brother and afraid of becoming implicated, he scattered his wealth among the poor and went into the mountains to seek the Way of Enlightenment. Finally, he was immortalized with the help of Han Zhongli and Lü Dongbin. Another source says that he left his mortal remains at a Taoist temple in Xuzhou.

The Eight were called the "roaming immortals" in Taoist legends. Their images appear in all sorts of arts and crafts, including furniture, chinaware, paintings and embroideries, often to convey the idea of a leisurely, carefree life.

The best known episode that involves all of them together is called *Ba Xian Guo Hai* or *The Eight Immortals Cross the Sea*. It describes how, when crossing a sea in their wanderings, each of them used a different object (a walking cane, a fan, a scimitar, etc.) as a vessel. This has given rise to an everyday saying: when people try to accomplish the same task by different methods, they are said to be emulating the example of the Eight Immortals crossing the sea.

They should not be confused with the "Eight Immortals of the Winecup" *(Yin Zhong Ba Xian)*. The latter are eight well-known poets of the Tang dynasty who used to drink together since they were just as fond of wine as they were devoted to poetry.

THE WHITE SNAKE

白蛇傳 *(Baishe Zhuan)*

A Chinese mythical tale of wide appeal is that of the White Snake. There are four characters in it — Bai Suzhen, Xiaoqing, Xu Xian and Fahai.

Suzhen is a white snake thousands of years old and, having acquired transcendant powers through self-cultivation, changes herself into a beautiful woman. Xiaoqing, her maid, is a green snake who has likewise assumed the form of a girl. Bored by the lonesome life in the mountains, they go to visit the beautiful city of Hangzhou.

They are caught in the rain at the side of West Lake near the Broken Bridge. Here they are offered an umbrella by Xu Xian, a young shopkeeper at the apothecary's in town. Suzhen (also known as the White Lady) falls in love with him and asks him to call on her the next day to get back his umbrella.

At their next meeting, their mutual admiration quickly blossoms into marriage. They live happily together for a few months until Xu Xian meets Fahai, Abbot of Jinshan Monastery.

This crafty, meddlesome hypocrite, jealous of the happiness of the lay world, tells Xu Xian that he has fallen into the trap of a demon and that his life is in danger.

At length, instigated by the wicked monk, Xu Xian goes home and plies the White Lady with a medicated wine till drunkenness makes her resume her original form. The sight sends Xu Xian into shock and a lasting stupor.

To save her husband, the White Lady goes up the Kunlun Mountains to steal a divine cure-all herb at the risk of her life. With tender care and Xiaoqing's assistance, she nurses Xu Xian back to health. But the loving yet apprehensive Xu Xian is abducted by Fahai and detained in the monastery.

An open, fierce struggle unfolds, culminating in the White Lady besieging Jinshan Monastery with a flood. She is defeated because she is in the advanced stages of pregnancy and has to run for her life with Xiaoqing. In the meantime, Xu Xian also escapes from the monastery.

Husband and wife meet once again at the Broken Bridge. The White Lady's love triumphs over her disappointment in the weak-willed behaviour of her husband and over the fiery temper of Xiaoqing, who wants to punish the ungrateful Xu Xian severely. The couple make up and live quietly in a nearby town until the birth of their baby.

The relentless Fahai tracks them down and, despite the infant's wails and the husband's entreaties, traps the White Lady and imprisons her under power of black magic in Leifeng Pagoda not far from West Lake.

Xiaoqing escapes but returns many years afterwards to burn down the pagoda and save her mistress.

The Story of the White Snake, which reflects the young people's longing for free love under the yoke of feudalism, has been a popular theme for many *genres* of art and literature — fiction, the stage and a great variety of handicraft. One of the mural paintings at the new Beijing International Airport illustrates this well-known story in a distinctively original style.

The setting of this fascinating story never fails to interest visitors to Hangzhou, but the ruins of Leifeng Pagoda are nowhere to be found. The pagoda in actual life was not burned down as told by the story but dilapidated and vanished. The local people, it is said, hating it as the prison of the gentle White Lady, made no effort to maintain it.

As to Jinshan Monastery, scene of the fighting between the monk and the "Snake Beauty" and itself a spot of tourist interest, it is located at the town of Zhenjiang in neighbouring Jiangsu province.

CHANG'E FLIES TO THE MOON

嫦娥奔月 *(Chang'e Ben Yue)*

Houyi (see further on the story *Houyi She Ri*), seeking perpetual youth, obtained the elixir of immortality from Xi Wangmu of the Kunlun Mountains. Returning to his palace, he confided the good news to his wife Chang'e, a lady graceful of carriage and unparalleled in beauty, very much loved by her husband.

One day, when Houyi was out, Chang'e secretly swallowed the potion in the hope that she would become immortal. The result was quite unexpected: she felt herself becoming light, so light that she flew up in spite of herself, drifting and floating in the air, until she reached the palace on the moon.

She is regarded by later generations as the goddess of the moon.

This beautiful story has always been liked by the Chinese and provides a favourite allusion for poets and writers. And in many occasions, the image of this beautiful lady, dressed in elegant traditional costumes and floating towards the moon, is used as the theme of the works of artists and sculptors.

THE FISHERMAN'S REVENGE

打漁殺家 *(Da Yu Sha Jia)*

Xiao En, a fearsome hero of the greenwood, retired from the business in his old age and wanted to live a simple life as a fisherman together with his young daughter Guiying. Both were good at martial arts.

In the county where they lived and fished, the magistrate had illegally relegated the collection of fishing tax to Squire Ding, a despotic landlord, who tried to squeeze all he could out of the poor fishermen.

The season had been so dry and water in the river so shallow that it was difficult to make any catches. However, a lackey of the Squire's still kept going the rounds to press for payment of tax. One day he happened to come when Xiao was in his boat with two well-known figures of the world of brave men, whom he had just met. These champions of the weak, furious on hearing about the extortions, spoke roughly to the tax-collector and told him to convey this message to his master: the squire had better behave himself or else he would come to grief.

Ding, angered by this warning, ordered his group of hired roughnecks to go to Xiao En's cottage to press for money by force and to teach him a lesson. This caused a fracas in front of the house. The hirelings, though superior in number, were actually sham fighters, and in the end they were sent fleeing helter-skelter. Their ring-leader was properly battered by father and daughter.

Xiao En felt he had better go and state his case before the magistrate. But the latter, as a friend of the squire's and with a fat bribe from him already in his pocket, ordered Xiao to be flogged without listening to a single word from him. On top of this, he ordered Xiao to go to kowtow to the landlord at his mansion by way of apology.

This was asking too much of Xiao En, who had been a knight errant, a sort of Robin Hood in his younger days. To add insult to injury was to drive him mad. Back home, he told his daughter Guiying that he had made up his mind to go right away that evening to the squire's to avenge himself. He told her to flee and to look for an old friend of his, to whose son Guiying had been betrothed since childhood.

Guiying will not let her father go out alone on this dangerous undertaking. She wants to be with him. They leave the house unlocked since it is to be deserted. In the dark they locate their fishing boat on the shore. Half way across the river Guiying feels a pang of fear and is mildly chided by her father. Finally, father and daughter pluck up their courage, force their way into the landlord's house, kill him and flee — back to the greenwood.

This story is presented as a Peking opera. The figures of white-bearded Xiao En and attractive Guiying are often seen in various handicraft works. The fisherman and his daughter in a boat symbolize the struggle of the common people against feudal oppression.

YU THE GREAT SUBDUES THE FLOOD

大禹治水 *(Da Yu Zhi Shui)*

It is not clearly known how many years passed after Nüwa had patched up the sky with melted coloured stones (Cf. *Nüwa Bu Tian*) when trouble broke out again. Gonggong, God of Water and Thunder, defeated in a power struggle against Zhuanxu, knocked himself against Buzhou Mountain in a burst of anger. The pillars on that Mountain which supported the vault of heaven broke again. As a result, heaven tilted to the northwest and the sun, the moon and the stars were set in motion, while the earth sank in the southwest, causing a great flood. Once more, great misery befell the people.

A super-man by the name of Gün, in commiseration with the sufferings of the people, tried to contain the flood. He stole God's "inexhaustible earth" with which to block the water and dam it up. Not only did he fail, but for his offence, he was executed by God's order. After his death, Yu, our hero, was born out of his abdomen.

When Yu grew up, he carried on his father's unfulfilled task, fighting against the Great Flood in the face of untold difficulties. For thirteen arduous years he travelled everywhere, devoting himself so conscientiously to his work that "wind was his hair-comb and rainfall his bath" and "three times he passed the door of his house without going in".

Drawing a lesson from his father's failure, he used methods of channelling and dredging and finally succeeded in subduing the Great Flood. He did so much for the people that the reigning Emperor Shun asked him to take over the throne. (Incidentally, his son Qi became the second emperor of the first hereditary dynasty, the Xia, by which name China is still occasionally referred to by writers in the classical style.)

Yu the Great is the personification of wisdom, perseverance and selfless devotion and, as such, he makes a popular theme for artistic creations.

AN UNREQUITED KINDNESS

東郭先生與中山狼 *(Dongguo Xian-sheng yu Zhongshan Lang)*

The fable of *The Wolf of Zhongshan* has been attributed to various authors of the Tang, the Song and the Ming dynasties, but the happenings are simple and consistent. It runs as follows:

Master Dongguo, a pedantic teacher and follower of Mohism, was ready to help anyone in distress, whosoever he might be and regardless of the circumstances. One day on a journey through Zhongshan Mountain, he came across a wounded wolf being pursued by the hunting party of the Viscount Zhao Jianzi. At bay, the wolf glibly and fawningly begged the master to help him. The old man saw a chance to act on the Mohist doctrine of "universal fraternity". At the risk of incurring the displeasure of the nobleman, he took the books out of his travelling bag and put the wolf in. When the Viscount came along and enquired if he had seen a wolf in flight, Master Dongguo lied, saying that he had noticed nothing unusual. The hunters galloped on.

However, when the wolf was let out of the bag, he showed his true features. He said he was hungry; since the master was so kind as to have helped him once, he might as well do it again by allowing himself to be eaten. Furthermore, he had been nearly suffocated in that beg a little while before, and that gave him another reason to avenge himself on the poor master. Now it was Master Dongguo's turn to take to his heels.

An old man came along leaning on a staff and asked what was the matter. Master Dongguo and the wolf gave their respective arguments and asked him to make a judgement. The old man thought over the situation for a few moments and said, "Mister Wolf should go back into the bag and if he is really tormented, then Master Dongguo should be eaten by him."

The wolf got into the bag again and it was tied up as before.

"What are you waiting for?" the old man asked Dongguo.

"Why don't you kill him right now?"

Only then did the master wake up to reality. And the wolf was put to death.

This fable is so well known among the Chinese that "Master Dongguo" is a synonym for a pedantic person and the "Wolf of Zhongshan" for an ingrate. And creations of handicraft art based on this theme, as they occasionally are, serve as constant reminders that the incorrigibly wicked are not to be appeased.

THE GODDESS OF MERCY

觀音 *(Guanyin)* or 觀世音 *(Guanshiyin)*

This is one of the principal Bodhisattvas of the Mahayana (Great Vehicle) School of Buddhism, originally called Avalokitesava in Sanskrit.

It is believed that when Buddhism was introduced to China, this deity was probably blended with a goddess of a certain Chinese faith or legend and assumed the form of a woman in people's mind as well as in statues and portraits. She came to be called Guanshiyin or Guanyin. Later, as a free translation, she was known popularly among the foreign communities and western visitors as the Goddess of Mercy.

Like the Bodhisattva Mahasthamaprapta, she is placed by the side of Amitabha Buddha on the dais of a Buddhist temple. The trio are called "The Three Saints from Western Paradise".

According to a Chinese sutra, she has great compassion for human suffering. Men and women will be relieved of their distress provided only that they appeal to her name. She is said to have appeared in any one of 32 forms: with willow branches, with a halo, dressed in white, lying on a lotus, on the moonlit water, with a kindly expression, with palms pressed together, with a thousand hands and a thousand eyes, and so on.

As a religious statue, artisans in the old days preferred to mould her into a sedate, benevolent goddess with no anomalies.

She figures in many a classical novel and drama as a divinity full of mercy and compassion, ready to render help to any one the least bit deserving. She is usually depicted as possessing a holy beauty, with a fair complexion and crimson lips, elegant eyebrows and graceful eyes, an attractive hairdo and flowing garments, holding a horsetail duster in her right hand and a vase of sweet magic dew in her left. With a flick of the willow twigs she sprinkles the dew over the human world, relieving all mortal beings of their sufferings.

Her powers undoubtedly emanated from the imagination

of a world constantly troubled by natural disasters and social injustices, in which the distressed sought some divinity on whom to pin their hope.

As a work of art, she is portrayed as riding, sitting or standing on various animals: a tortoise, an elephant, a lion, a dragon or some other mythical beast. This stems from the various episodes in fiction and folklore, which have been woven about her personality.

AN IMPERIAL CONCUBINE GETS TIPSY

貴妃醉酒 *(Guifei Zui Jiu)*

When you visit Xi'an, your schedule will most probably include a tour to the nearby Lintong with its hot springs where, you will be told, the famous Yang Guifei used to take her baths.

Yang Guifei (719-756 A.D.) was one of those rare women in history like Helen of Troy whose beauty led to wars and nationwide troubles.

She was named Yang Taizhen, more often called Yuhuan (Jade Bracelet), and still more popularly known as Guifei, the last being her official title, i.e., Imperial Concubine of the Highest Rank.

As a child, she received an excellent musical training. At the age of fifteen, she was taken into the harem of the eighteenth prince of the Tang Emperor Xuan Zong (also known as Ming Huang). Three years later she somehow found herself in the palace of the emperor, who immediately made her his favourite. In the year 745 A.D., the title of Guifei was bestowed on her.

In a long narrative poem by the Tang poet Bai Juyi on her life and tragic end, she is said to "pale all the beauties of the six palace courts as she turns back with her smile of a hundred fascinations". In fact, she was so much in the imperial grace that all her three sisters were given ranks in the nobility and Yang Guozhong, a first cousin of hers, rose to prime ministership in spite of his incompetence in all fields except corruption and intrigue. As a result, administration of the country deteriorated, giving rise to chaos.

In 755 A.D., An Lushan, a local military governor, staged a revolt ostensibly against Yang Guozhong (and the romancers say, to get Yang Guifei). The imperial household had to flee Xi'an under military escort. When the party arrived at the Village of Mawei (west of present-day Xingping County in Shaanxi Province), the soldiers refused to go on. Blaming the Yangs for all the sufferings of the people, they insisted on settling accounts. Yang Guozhong was lynched by the discontented troops, and. Yang Guifei also had to be hanged before the soldiers were pacified.

After the country was once more under control, the emperor abdicated and spent his remaining years reminiscing of his favourite concubine.

Many works of art in various forms — poems, romances, plays, paintings, sculptures, etc. — have been created with Yang Guifei as the subject. Some simply portray her beauty, while others picture scenes from her life, for instance, *Guifei Takes a Bath (Guifei Chu Yu)*, *The Palace of Perpetual Youth (Chang Sheng Dian)* which depicts an oath-taking love scene between the emperor and his favourite concubine, *Tang Ming Huang Visits the Moon Palace (You Yue Gong)* in search of his departed Guifei, etc. There is also a play on her whole life entitled *The Unofficial Biography of Taizhen (Taizhen Wai Zhuan)*.

Mei Lanfang, the celebrated impersonator of women's roles in Peking Opera, used to present a lyrical one-act play called *The Drunken Beauty* or *An Imperial Concubine Gets Tipsy (Guifei Zui Jiu)*. The story is very simple: it relates that even the special favourtie now and then may have a lonesome evening when the emperor spends the night with his empress or one of the other concubines. It is on one such evening that Guifei, waiting in vain for a visit from the emperor, takes herself one cup too many and sings to the moon, the flowers and the birds of her disappointment, her jealousy and the fickleness of human sentiments. This theme is widely used by other forms of art.

HONGXIAN STEALS A GOLD BOX

紅線盜盒 *(Hongxian Dao He)*

The once-flourishing Tang dynasty began to decline with the revolt of An Lushan (see *Guifei Zui Jiu*), although this was quelled in the end.

An Lushan had been one of the military satraps. These were high-ranking military governors vested with both administrative and military powers over large regions of the country. The system of satraps was originally established for the purpose of consolidating the Tang rule, but with central authority on the wane the satraps became virtually independent. While some remained loyal to the throne, others began to become overweeningly ambitious.

Tian Chengsi, satrap of Weibo area which covers parts of present-day Shandong, Hebei and Henan provinces, was one of those obsessed with consuming ambition. As a first step, he proposed to annex Luzhou area (covering 10 counties of present-day Shanxi and an adjoining part of Hebei province). To this end, he recruited a large private army, which included 3,000 specially-trained troops.

Now Governor Xue Song, the military satrap of Luzhou, was faithful to the court and had been given power of jurisdiction over extensive regions on both sides of the Yellow River by imperial edict. Superior to Tian in the feudal hierarchy but inferior in armed strength, he was at a loss what to do when news of Tian's sinister preparations reached him.

He had a young maid-servant called Hongxian, who was well read in history and classics, conversant with music and, what is more, well-trained in martial arts. Learning one evening about the dangerous situation in which her master found himself, she immediately offered her help. Losing no time, she went inside her room to change. She came out, clad in a short embroidered purple overcoat, silk socks and light boots, with a magic incantation on her forehead.

She left the satrap during the first watch of the evening and returned at mid-night. She had gone to Weibo, covering a round trip of three hundred and fifty kilometres in a few hours, and had stolen a gold box containing conclusive evidence of the satrap Tian Chengsi's conspiracy against the state.

The next day, Xue Song despatched a messenger with a letter to return the gold box to Tian Chengsi. Startled, Tian realized that there must be some person of extraordinary abilities under Xue Song's command, a person who could gain easy access to his well-guarded secret and consequently could also endanger his life. He thought it better to disband his forces and write back to Xue Song, pledging his friendship and homage. He remained quiet for some time to come.

The story, praising the chivalrous action of a maid and upholding national unity, was written by a Tang author and has been used as the theme for various arts, including the Peking opera.

HOUYI SHOOTS DOWN THE SUNS

后羿射日 *(Houyi She Ri)*

Houyi, leader of a tribe and a superb archer, is one of the male heroes in Chinese mythology, like Yu the Great.

In the remote past, it is said, there were ten suns in the sky, veritable burning fires which scorched the plants, the grass and the woods. Nothing could grow and there was great famine. On top of this, snakes and beasts roamed everywhere, endangering the people.

In view of this, the Emperor Yao presented Houyi a strong bow and sharp arrows with orders to shoot down the suns and kill the beasts to rescue the people from their misery.

Houyi defied all difficulties to carry out this order, and succeeded in shooting down all the surplus suns and finishing off the ferocious animals. Since then, there has been only one sun shining in the sky, making for a temperate climate, exuberant vegetation, fine harvests and consequently general well-being. His immortal feats for the people and for posterity won Houyi universal admiration and support.

This popular myth symbolises the people's aspiration for power to bring the natural elements under control.

A PIONEER IN MEDICINE
華佗 *(Hua Tuo)*

Hua Tuo was a famous doctor who lived 1,700 years ago during the Three Kingdoms Period. He not only read widely but travelled extensively, practising medicine. His keen powers of observation, tireless penchant for research and ability to accurately sum up his experiences enabled him to perfect his healing art ceaselessly.

Like Bianque, a famous physician of the Warring States Period (403-221 B.C.), he had a talent for making diagnosis by observing the patients' outward symptoms. Once he found a group of people drinking in a tavern and was struck by the complexion of one of them. He went over to ask the man how he felt. The reply was that he felt quite alright, just as usual. Hua warned him that he was seriously ill and that he must not drink any more. The man died soon afterwards.

A versatile practitioner, he was expert in acupuncture. The discovery of *jiaji,* an acupoint on the spine frequently used today, is attributed to him. He wrote *Hua Tuo's Book on Acupuncture,* which remained one of the most authoritative works on the subject for many generations after his death.

One of his great contributions was the development of an oral anaesthetic for use in surgical operations. The prescription consists chiefly of datura blossoms and certain other wild poisonous herbs, all of which grow abundantly in China's southern regions. His method later spread to the Arab world.

A famous patient operated on by him was General Guan Yu (see stories from *The Romance of the Three Kingdoms).* In a battle Guan Yu had been injured in the arm by a lethally poisonous arrow. Invited to give treatment, Hua Tuo cut open the lesion and scraped the poison off the bone. All the while, the general went on playing chess without a wince. His wound soon healed and the patient suffered no disability whatever.

With the use of his oral anaesthetic, he is said to have performed many successful major operations involving internal organs. He must have had a fine grasp of anatomy and physiology.

He was also an early exponent of physical exercise for its curative and preventive value. By observing and imitating the movements of certain animals (like the tiger, bear, monkey and deer) and birds, he designed a set of callisthenics which he called "The Game of Five Animals". With this, he cured certain chronic diseases, notably disorders of the digestive system, and the game became quite popular in certain regions of the country already during his lifetime.

But this giant in Chinese medicine did not come to a happy end. Called in by Cao Cao, the Prime Minister, to treat his migraine, the doctor relieved him of his pain instantly with the application of a single acupuncture needle at the effective point. Cao Cao wanted him to remain at court as his personal physician. Unwilling to spend his time in the service of a handful of people, Hua Tuo declined on the excuse of an ailing mother who needed his constant attention. When Cao Cao found out this was an evasion, he had him arrested and finally put to death.

While in prison, the doctor asked his gaoler to help smuggle his medical works to the outside world for the benefit of the people. Unable to persuade the gaoler, who was afraid to take the risk, Hua Tuo committed his works to the flames. This was a great loss to the medical heritage of the country.

THE GENERAL RECONCILED WITH THE CHIEF MINISTER

將相和 *(Jiang Xiang He)*

In the latter half of the Warring States Period (403-221 B.C.), the state of Qin was expanding in the west and threatening the other neighbouring regions.

It came to the knowledge of the Qin monarch that the king of Zhao was in possession of a precious jade emblem. He sent a message to Zhao offering to exchange fifteen cities for this coveted object. It was clearly a trick, and the king of Zhao was thrown into a quandary, for to refuse would constitute an affront to a powerful neighbour, while to agree would mean giving up the rare treasure without getting the cities in return.

A petty official — in fact, a retainer of an influential court eunuch — by the name of Lin Xiangru volunteered to go to Qin with the jade to negotiate the matter, promising that he would have the "jade returned intact to Zhao" unless he could take possession of the fifteen cities as promised.

Sima Qian, the celebrated Han dynasty historian, has written the following dramatic passage about how Lin acquitted himself at the Qin court:

Seeing that the king did not mean to give Zhao the cities, Xiangru stepped forward and said: "There is a flaw in this jade. Let me show it to Your Majesty." When the king handed him the jade, he took his stand with his back against a pillar. His hair bristled with rage and he cried: ". . . As Your Majesty has no intention of giving these cities to Zhao, I have taken back the jade. Try to get it from me by force, and I shall break both my head and the jade against this pillar!" With a glance at the pillar he held up the jade, and made ready to smash it.

Lin Xiangru's courage and patriotism impressed the king of Qin, who let him go back to Zhao with the jade emblem and without harming him.

This episode is popularly known among the Chinese as *Wan Bi Gui Zhao (Jade Returned Intact to Zhao)*.

This setback rankled, and the powerful king of Qin tried again to humiliate the king of Zhao.

At a banquet during a conference in Mianchi in the year 279 B.C., he complimented the king of Zhao on his musical talents and asked him to play on the zither. The latter complied reluctantly. When he had finished, the king of Qin turned to his official historian, saying, "put down in the annals that on such and such a date the king of Zhao played on the zither to entertain His Majesty the Great King of Qin."

Lin Xiangru, who was with his liege, grew furious. He took up an earthern pot and knelt before the king of Qin, complimented him also on his musical talents and asked him to play on the pot. When the latter turned red with anger, Lin continued, ". . . or else my uncouth blood might splash on Your Majesty within this short distance of five feet!" The king of Qin had to strike once with his chopsticks on the pot. Thereupon, turning to the Zhao historian, Lin said, "Please record it in the annals that the king of Qin played on the earthern pot to amuse His Majesty the Great King of Zhao."

So Qin was again frustrated in its attempt to humiliate Zhao, thanks once more to the courage and ingenuity of Lin Xiangru, who was now backed also by the war-preparedness mounted by General Lian Po of Zhao.

These events explain why Lin Xiangru rose from his obscure origin to become chief minister of the state, a position higher than all others except that of the king himself. This aroused the displeasure of General Lian Po who had distinguished himself as the commander of several big victorious battles during a long military career and had won nation-wide acclaim.

The elderly warrior set his mind on slighting the chief minister on every possible occasion and he made no secret of his intentions. When they met on a narrow street with their respective processions, the general would not make way for his superior, the chief minister. At this, Lin would turn back to take another route. Sometimes he would absent himself from court on plea of illness in order to avoid meeting the general. This show of timidity was only too apparent; his followers protested. The chief minister explained to them:

Mighty as he is, I bellowed at the king of Qin in his own court and defied his ministers. Why then should I fear General Lian, weak though I am? Understand — the two of us are the only reason why powerful Qin dare not invade Zhao. If two tigers fight, one must perish. I take this stand because I put our country first and private grudges second.

When this became known to the king of Zhao, he instructed one of his ministers to mediate between the two. The magnanimous words of Lin Xiangru moved the patriotic general. At his earliest convenience he paid a visit to the chief minister's mansion, carrying birch-rods on his bare back, knelt down before Lin to express his heart-felt apologies and asked for a flogging. Lin also knelt down. The two great statesmen shed tears of happiness mixed with remorse, and from then on became the best of friends, united in their common will to defend the interests of their country.

JINGWEI FILLING UP THE SEA

精衛填海 *(Jingwei Tian Hai)*

Nüwa*, daughter of Emperor Yan in pre-historic China, drowned in the sea while swimming. Her ghost, according to an ancient myth, resolved to avenge her death by filling up the sea.

Her spirit changed itself into a small bird with a multi-coloured head, white bill, red feet and black feathers. As she flew she chirped *"jingwei, jingwei"*, which became her name.

All she did, day and night, was carry pebbles and things in her bill from the West Mountain and drop them into the East Sea in an unremitting effort to fill it up.

She is still at it, if the myth is to be believed. For the sea is still there.

The staunch little bird has been sung by great poets of past ages and repeatedly depicted by artists of various genres down to this day. The story of *Jingwei Tian Hai* has become an inspiring symbol of dogged determination.

* Not to be confused with Nüwa who repaired heaven.

GOD OF LONGEVITY

老壽星 *(Lao Shouxing)*

This figure of an old man is frequently seen in paintings, porcelain wares, and sculptures, which were often used as birthday presents, as it symbolises the human wish for a long life. But there are different interpretations as to who the god was.

One version says that he was Laozi, *alias* Li Dan, who was already three hundred years old at the beginning of the Zhou dynasty (11th century B.C.) and who served as official historian to the throne for 276 years. Another source claims that he was born even before heaven and earth were created and lived through the ages of the "Three Sovereigns and Five Emperors" down to the Zhou dynasty. Yet a third source records simply that he was a native of Kuxian county in the state of Chu during the Spring and Autumn Period.

All accounts, however, seem to agree on his appearance and character. He is distinguished by an abnormally large, protruding forehead which is deeply lined and crowned with white hair; also by big ears, long eyebrows, and a square mouth with thick lips. He had a quiet and tranquil character, indifferent to fame and gain, free from cares and worries. He was in favour of everything following its natural course, and opposed to all expressions of affectation and artificiality. In the running of a state, he advocated doing nothing that went against nature. He is said to have sought and studied the way of Illumination in the Kunlun Mountains. He wrote the *Daode Jing*, a Taoist classic, and was later considered to be the founder of Taoism.

As he lived an almost interminable long life, he has been popularly known as "Laozi" (the very old one) or "Lao Shouxing" (the old undying star), the Chinese name for the star Canopus.

Another version says Lao Shouxing was a totally different man by the name of Peng, generally known as Peng Zu or Old Man Peng. This legend claims that at the end of the Shang dynasty (11th century B.C.) he was already 767 years old but showed no signs of senility. He is also said to be of a quiet nature, not interested in worldly affairs but devoted to physical self-cultivation.

When offered a high government post by the King, he declined it. On the pretext of illness, he managed to keep himself out of officialdom and politics. A stay-at-home, he rarely ventured out, and when on occasion he did, he would go on foot and alone, wandering about without any definite aim or destination.

He developed a whole set of indoor exercises — meditation, deep-breathing and massage — not only to keep fit but to cure himself of occasional ailments or feelings of discomfort. When kings and princes asked him to teach them the secret of long life, he would refuse; their donations of gold and jewelry, he would accept, passing them on to the needy and poor without keeping any for himself.

He said he had no father when he was born, lost his mother when he was three, lived through more than a century of war, chaos and exile in the western region, and survived 49 wives and 54 sons. Not entirely free from sorrows and troubles, he complained that was why he had died "young" at the age of eight hundred years, when his life was cut short after only a brief span.

The name "Peng Zu" came to be synonymous with "longevity" in later ages.

Both versions, though equally preposterous, were accepted without question by the credulous populace throughout the ages as authentic accounts of the origin of the God of Longevity. Nowadays, painters and sculptors just take the old man as a theme on which to give rein to their imaginative creation.

THE FOOLISH OLD MAN

老愚公 *(Lao Yugong)*

This is the hero in an ancient Chinese fable entitled *Yugong Yi Shan (The Foolish Old Man Removed the Mountains),* first recorded in an ancient work of the Period of the Warring States.

He was an old man of ninety, says the fable, who lived in northern China and was known as the Foolish Old Man of North Mountain. His house faced south and beyond his doorway stood two great mountains, Taihang and Wangwu, obstructing the way. He made up his mind to remove these mountains. After consulting with his wife, he led his family members to take up their hoes, set about digging the rocks and earth of the two mountains and moving them away basketful by basketful, with shoulder-poles. They worked hard in the midst of great difficulties.

Another greybeard, known as the Wise Old Man, saw them and laughed at them, remarking that it was foolish of them to have taken up this impossible feat. How could they, a handful of people, remove two big mountains?

The Foolish Old Man replied, "When I die, my sons will carry on; when they die, there will be my grandsons, and then their sons and grandsons; and so on, forever. High as they are, the mountains cannot grow any higher, and with every bit we dig, they will be that much lower. Why can't we clear them away?"

With this refutation of the Wise Old Man's erroneous view, he turned back to his digging and went on every day, unshaken in his conviction. God, moved by this, sent down two angels to carry the mountains away on their backs.

LIANG SHANBO AND ZHU YINGTAI

梁山伯與祝英台
(Liang Shanbo yu Zhu Yingtai)

In China one may chance to hear a violin concerto of the same title. The instruments used are western but the style and theme distinctively Chinese. This combination you will most probably find highly enjoyable.

The story, which hinges on the love-tragedy of a young couple, is also presented from time to time on the stage by various types of Chinese opera.

Yingtai was the daughter and only child of Squire Zhu. She wanted to go to school and get an education, which in old China was almost the sole right of boys whose families could afford it. She prevailed upon her father who, in a moment of doting fondness, agreed that she might go to study under a well-known tutor in the guise of a young man, accompanied by a maid, disguised as "his" page.

She stayed away from home for three years and studied at a private school run by a single tutor. While there she fell hopelessly in love with one of her few schoolmates, Liang Shanbo, who never for a moment suspected that she was a girl.

The day of parting came at the end of her three-year term. Yingtai, revealing her true identity to the master's wife (who had all along suspected as much), asked her to be the match-maker for her and Shanbo when the opportunity should present itself.

Shanbo accompanied her on the short journey out of the mountain in which the school was situated, in order to bid her farewell on the main road. Along the way, Yingtai repeatedly hinted about her love for him by comparing their relationship to that between love-birds, flowers sharing the same stem, pairs of fish swimming in the stream . . . But the naive Shanbo laughed at her for using inadequate similes. In the end, Yingtai told him that she had a younger sister at home whom she would like to introduce to him, but he must make haste and come before a certain festival to press his suit.

Back at school, the master's wife told Shanbo the truth about Yingtai. Shanbo lost no time in going after her.

In the meantime, during Yingtai's absence, her father had betrothed her to a young man of a wealthy and influential family by the name of Ma, whom Yingtai had never met. She was stricken with grief by the news and told her father about the young man who had won her heart. All pleas and entreaties were of no avail; the father who had been indulgent about her seeking an education in disguise was now adamant. A breach of the engagement would be unthinkable, for it would mean a scandal, a loss of face — that the daughter of a respectable family should have chosen her own husband and that in spite of her father!

So when Shanbo arrived on the scene, all that Yingtai could get from her father was the permission to meet him for a few minutes. At their brief meeting, she told him what had happened and the young couple poured out their grief and despair to each other in heart-rending songs and tears of disappointment.

Shanbo went away broken-hearted and soon died of melancholy at home.

The sad news reached Yingtai just before the appointed date of her wedding to young Ma. She agreed to go to the bridegroom's house only on condition that on the way she be allowed to stop at the tomb of Shanbo to mourn his death. The father had no alternative but to acquiesce.

At Shanbo's grave, Yingtai ordered the bridal procession to stop, got down from the palanquin and took off her red wedding gown. Under it was a second dress, all white, the colour of mourning in old China. She lamented the death of Shanbo and their sad fate. In her anguish, she rushed headlong towards the tomb-stone and was killed instantly. The tomb opened up and took Yingtai inside.

From time to time in after-years a pair of large butterflies could be seen over the grave fluttering happily among the flowers. People say they are reincarnations of Shanbo and Yingtai.

AN INGENIOUS CRAFTSMAN

魯班 *(Lu Ban)*

In the old days, Lu Ban was considered to be the founder and patron saint of the building trade.

He lived and worked in the 5th century B.C. during the last years of the Spring and Autumn Period and already in his own lifetime became far and wide known for his great ingenuity as an artisan. He is said to have been the inventor of many carpenter's tools, including the saw, the planer, the ink marker, the drill, etc. Most of these are still being used today. The stone mill is also credited to him.

His name lived on and many interesting episodes about him have been passed on by word of mouth and enjoyed with great relish by the people throughout the ages. Most of them are very instructive and thought-provoking, though some may be out and out legends.

For instance, his leg was once cut by a kind of weed while working. He noticed that the weed had sawteeth on the edges. This is how he thought of making the first saw in China.

Once he carved a phoenix. The result was so life like that when it was finished it flew away. On another occasion, a wooden bird made by him stayed in the air for three days.

Then, there is the story about a stone block he chiselled for a kindly poor widow. He knew a bridge-builder nearby would need the block at the last moment to complete his bridge before the deadline and enough money would be paid to the widow for it to provide her daughter with a dowry.

Another legend about him goes like this: The Prince of a certain state wanted to have some corner towers added to his palace and demanded that each tower should have nine beams, eighteen pillars and seventy-two ridges. Failure to satisfy his fancy led to the execution of several master-builders. Now the order to build the towers was given to a young artisan whose father had just lost his life in this way. The young man was driven to distraction by this impossible job and was about to commit suicide when he was stopped by Lu Ban who happened to be passing by. He told the young

55

man never to despair but to keep on looking for a solution. At least he should wait three days to see if he, Lu Ban, could help him.

Lu Ban, who had no ready-made answer either, brooded over the problem for two days. On the third, he saw a small boy selling katydids in tiny cages. This gave him an idea! For the rest of the day and night he tried manipulaïing sorghum stalks until, by the next morning, he had produced a bird-cage of very complicated and magnificent structure. He had the model sent to the discouraged building artisan who examined it carefully. Sure enough, on counting the parts, he found — 9 beams, 18 pillars and 72 ridges!

Lu Ban, the symbol of industriousness, thoughtfulness and ingenuity, always makes a good subject for painters, sculptors and other artists, carrying with it the eternal message that wisdom comes from labour to those who think hard enough.

THE NYMPH OF THE RIVER LUO

洛神 *(Luo Shen)*

Luo Shen is a mythical figure of ancient China. She became popularly known because of a poem, *Ode to the Nymph of the River Luo (Luo Shen Fu)*, composed by Cao Zhi of the Three Kingdoms period.

It is said that she was Mifei, the daughter of Emperor Fuxi of prehistorical legends, and became a nymph after she was drowned in the Luo River. (This river flows through Shaanxi and Henan provinces and the tourist town of Luoyang.)

A goddess of peerless beauty, she is, in the words of Cao Zhi's poem, as "elegant as a startled swan and supple as a swimming dragon." Light of carriage and attractive in appearance, she looks from a distance like the red sun carried up by the morning glow and, from nearby, like the lotus freshly borne out by the clear waters. She is of medium height and stature, between plump and thin, slender of shoulders and waist, fair and clear in complexion. Her tresses are coiffured like clouds over a pair of long, graceful brows. She has white teeth inside a pair of crimson lips. With eyes limpid as autumn waters, her face carries a faint smile vaguely suggested by her dimples. Refined in bearing, she is gentle and tender. Attired in a gorgeous costume and swaying skirt of silk gauze, she is crowned with a gold coronet set off by jade ornaments, radiating magnificence and fragrance. On an excursion outside her palace gates she is flanked by colourful banners and fluttering standards and followed by a cortege of graceful ladies-in-waiting, she rides in a cloud-borne chariot drawn by a team of six dragons, with sea birds hovering about in escort.

She seems to be going ahead, or is it that she has stopped and wants to turn back? She appears about to say something but has not yet uttered a word. Looking around, she is full of a subtle longing and affection.

A personality unparalleled on earth or in heaven, she is as tantalizing as she is divinely beautiful.

It is in an effort to catch this grace, this subtle, exquisite quality that artists have used her as the theme for paintings, shell carving pictures, inlaid or carved screens. Their masterly execution generally succeeds in winning appreciation.

MAGU PRESENTS HER BIRTHDAY GIFT

麻姑獻壽 *(Magu Xian Shou)*

Magu is a goddess in a well-known ancient myth.

Having attained Illumination on a mountain near Mouzhou, she came to the human world during the reign of Emperor Huan in the Eastern Han dynasty. Although she appeared to be a young maiden of eighteen or nineteen, yet according to her own account, she had lived long enough to witness personally three metamorphoses in which the East Sea turned into mulberry groves and then changed back into the sea again. From this was born the Chinese expression *canghai sangtian* ("blue seas and mulberry groves") meaning that time brings about great vicissitudes in the world.

She was described as a beauty with a chignon on top of her head and the rest of the hair hanging down to her waist. Her dress was shiny and colourfully patterned. One incongruous version of the original myth says that she had talon-like hands, which led some contemporary, supposed to have seen her, to think "they must be good for scratching itches."

She commanded supernatural powers and could change rice grains into pearls by throwing them up in the air.

On the third day of the third moon, the birthday of Xi Wangmu (Cf. article under that title), she was invited by four other fairy maidens to go with them to attend the celebration, and she brought along the divine wine she had brewed of a magic herb with the water from the Crimson-Pearl River that imparts perpetual health. At the party, she and the other girls presented choral and dance performances to express their best wishes to the hostess.

In the old days, therefore, paintings of Magu (the artists, as a rule, carefully forgot about the talon-hands) were frequently used as birthday presents to elderly ladies.

MENG JIANGNU WEEPS AT THE GREAT WALL

孟姜女哭長城
(Meng Jiangnü Ku Changcheng)

If you go sightseeing to the Great Wall, you should know this legend, especially if your visit is at Shanhaiguan. It will remind you that the wall is not only one of the wonders of the world, a gigantic work of man, but the result of despotism and forced labour.

In the days of the First Emperor of the Qin dynasty (221-206 B.C.), it is said, Meng Jiangnü's young husband Fan Xiliang was drafted for the building of the Great Wall up in the north. Hearing no word from him for a long time, she decided to take him some winter clothes and travelled from their hometown Tongguan of Shaanxi province for thousands of miles to Shanhaiguan, the pass between North China and the Northeast.

Arriving there, she searched in vain for her husband among the thousands of forced labourers. After a long time, she came to learn that Xiliang, like so many others, had died of hardship and overwork and had been buried somewhere under the wall.

Overcome with sorrow, she wept at the Great Wall for days on end. Her grief was so overwhelming that the gods were moved. A part of the wall collapsed, revealing the remains of her husband.

She plunged into the sea to end her life.

At Shanhaiguan, where the eastern end of the Great Wall meets the sea, there are today certain relics in memory of Meng Jiangnü:

- A temple and statue dedicated to her memory, with inscriptions written in her praise by famous personages of various dynasties. This is about four miles to the east of the present town.
- A big rock nearby which, supposedly, she climbed up every day, looking for her husband, and on which she wore out still-visible marks of her footsteps.
- Two offshore rocks, said to have risen out of the sea to mark the place where she drowned herself, one re-

sembling a tomb, the other a monument.

The tale of Meng Jiangnü, the faithful, loving wife who opposed tyranny, made its appearance during the Tang dynasty.

HUA MULAN

木蘭從軍 *(Mulan Cong Jun)*

Among the works of sculpture, whether in jade, stone or ivory, you might see a youth of great beauty attired in the full regalia of an ancient general. This is most probably the intrepid Hua Mulan, a girl who joined the army as a man.

The earliest praises of Mulan are found in an anonymous epic of the Northern Dynasties (386-581 A.D.). Later folk story-tellers and playwrights gave her a surname (Hua) and wove various details about her adventures to bring them to life.

According to one version, Hua Hu who had served in the army with an outstanding record was now old and in poor health, although his name still remained on the list of the reserves. One day, he received an urgent mobilisation order because of a highly critical situation at the northern border brought on by repeated foreign incursions. His second daughter Mulan who first took the message was set to thinking . . . How could Father go at his age? This was out of the question. The only other male in the family was her brother who was too young for military service. The call, however, had to be answered by someone. She made up her mind to enlist disguised as a young man, using her brother's name.

She prevailed upon her parents, who of course did not agree at first.

On her way to the front, she met with a few other draftees, all headed for the border garrison. But before being formally enlisted, they were drawn into the fight by battle cries. It turned out that the commander of the border troops was surrounded by the enemy. From the very beginning, Mulan distinguished herself in extricating the marshal from his impasse.

From then on, she rendered one meritorious service after another until, 12 years afterwards, she was promoted to be a general without anyone suspecting her of being a woman. In the meantime, the contending forces remained locked in a stalemate.

One night, as Mulan was personally making a round of inspection, she heard the fluttering of wild birds in the north. It occurred to her at once that they must have been startled by the approaching enemy. This she reported to the marshal.

Disposition of troops was quickly made and an ambush laid for the enemy forces which had come out on a surprise night attack. The invaders were taken by surprise in a decisive engagement and wiped out, with their leader captured by Mulan. The border war ended in a victory, achieved in no small measure through the outstanding exploits of Mulan.

The Chinese forces returned in triumph. Imperial honours were showered on Mulan. Instead of accepting the high official post offered her, she begged leave to go home to aid and comfort her parents in their old age.

Meanwhile, the marshal who entertained a grateful admiration and a growing fondness for his young general offered his only daughter in marriage. Mulan had to find one excuse after another to put off the matter.

Unconvinced, the marshal paid a personal visit to Mulan at her cottage with an entourage of her former comrades-in-arms to press the match. When they discovered her to be a pretty woman, their surprise was as immense as their admiration.

Mulan, throughout the ages, has been held up by the Chinese people as a symbol of patriotism, a paragon of filial piety, and a woman of outstanding valour and heroism.

NEZHA CREATES AN UPROAR IN THE SEA

哪吒鬧海 *(Nezha Nao Hai)*

Nezha is a household word in China. This is the name of a young mythological hero who turns the sea upside down.

According to one version of the tale, he first appears in the strange form of a huge egg, given birth to by the wife of General Li Jing, military governor of a region in ancient China. The father, exasperated at the sight, pulls out his sword to destroy the monstrous thing. The shell cracks open and, falling apart, reveals the bud of a lotus, which slowly opens its petals and, in its turn, unveils the tiny figure of Nezha, already running and jumping about.

While the general is marvelling at what he sees, the Venerable Master Taiyi, a celestial being, alights from heaven to call on him and, with the father's consent, takes the boy as his disciple and protégé. He teaches the baby the magic arts by whispering a few words into his ears and, before he leaves, gives him some magic weapons.

A few years later, when Nezha is about seven years old, the region is struck by a long drought and the crops are about to be destroyed by the heat. The people pray and offer sacrifices to the Dragon King, who rules from his crystal palaces a the bottom of the sea and is in charge of rain as his divine duty.

This greedy, ruthless ruler of the East Sea grumbles that he is fed up with the pigs and sheep offered by the people and has word passed around that he must have live lads and lasses for his meals before he will let a single drop of rain fall on earth. When no human sacrifice is forthcoming, the Dragon King becomes enraged and, his appetite whetted, sends forth his underlings to grab children.

Young Nezha is playing near the seashore. When he hears that a playmate of his has been seized, he gives chase and becomes embroiled in a fight with the Dragon King's third and favourite son, whom he kills.

The old King of the Sea comes to General Li to seek revenge. The General does not believe that his infant son

69

can have done a thing like that until he gets a corroborating account from the boy himself.

The Dragon King goes to Heaven to seek justice from the Supreme Sovereign of the whole universe. But he is waylaid by Nezha, who gives him a beating and makes him promise never to raise the issue again.

The promise, of course, is a false one made under duress. Once back in his palace, he sends for all three of his brothers, who are also Dragon Kings reigning respectively over the West, North and South Seas. Together they raise a horde of sea-monsters and lay siege to the palace of General Li. In the meantime, they order torrents of rains to pour down from the sky over the area for three days and nights. The people, who have suffered from drought, are now being drowned. The dragons threaten that they will not let up unless and until the general has his son put to death.

The general, for fear of more trouble, has had Nezha's magic weapons hidden away. This deprives the boy of his fighting prowess. The father, under the pressure of the cruel dragons and out of pity for the people's sufferings, wavers over sacrificing his son to appease the sea-monsters.

Seeing the impasse of his father, Nezha commits suicide with his father's sword.

The downpour lets up and the floods recede.

The soul of Nezha goes to his old master, bewailing his fate. The all-wise immortal quietly gathers together a flower, two leaves and some roots of the lotus, arranges them in the shape of a boy and, uttering an incantation, infuses the object with Nezha's soul. A new Nezha is reborn, one that looks exactly the same as before, but is not of human flesh and blood and is therefore invulnerable. Besides, the boy is told how to transform himself, when necessary, into a fighter with three heads and six arms so that he may battle many enemies at the same time. He also is given a magic spear and a pair of flaming wheels which carry him through the air in

70

flight.

He goes straight back to the under-water palaces of the Dragon King and engages all the sea-monsters in a violent battle, from which he emerges all-triumphant. Not only are the dragon's palaces levelled, but the enemies suffer a genuine surrender this time and vow that they will never harm the people again.

The Chinese people love this story, for to them it represents the triumph of freedom over tyranny, and of man over nature.

THE COWHERD AND THE GIRL WEAVER

牛郎織女 *(Niulang Zhinü)*

This is a story born out of star-gazing by the people of ancient times. It first appeared as one of a collection of folk poems more than 2,000 years ago. Its description of the tragic love affair between two stars, Altair and Vega, underwent later embellishments which developed it into a full-fledged fairy tale.

The Girl Weaver (Vega) is a granddaughter of the Ethereal Emperor, as clever as she is beautiful. She spends year after year in Heaven weaving beautiful brocades with the colourful clouds in the skies. Occasionally when she feels fatigued or bored by her work, she peeps down on earth. Once, she happens to see a young cowherd and takes a fancy to him.

This young man is the second of two brothers of a well-to-do family. When still quite young, they lose their parents. He lives with his elder brother and the latter's wife. The sister-in-law treats him badly, feeding him with the leftovers but giving him all the heavy work, which includes tending the ox. For this, he is simply called Cowherd. Good, honest and diligent by nature, he accepts whatever comes his way without suspecting any malice.

Even then, the sister-in-law is not satisfied but urges her husband to break up the household with Cowherd, intending to cheat him out of his share of the property.

Cowherd becomes very sad and one day, out with the ox, he weeps at the prospect of having to live away from his brother. Also he does not know what to do about the division of the family property. Suddenly the ox — not really an animal but a divinity in the shape of an ox — begins to talk. He says to Cowherd, "Don't fight for anything at the division of the property. Just ask to have me."

This is what Cowherd says to the selfish sister, which is far better than she has hoped for. So, the two brothers part without ado but with all the property — house, money, furniture, land, implements, other chattels — going to the elder one.

Contrary to the expectation of the sister-in-law, Cowherd manages to live quite well all alone, guided always by the advice of the old ox.

One evening, according to what the ox tells him, Cowherd goes to the riverside where he finds a group of young goddesses bathing in the river. He sneaks up to where they have left their clothes and steals a red dress from among them and goes into hiding nearby. When the fairy maidens come up from the river to put on their dresses again, one of them cries out that hers is missing. They look round for it in vain. But time is up and they have to return to Heaven. The one who has lost her dress has to remain behind, crying. And this is the Girl Weaver, most beautiful of them all.

Cowherd comes out from hiding and, with the intervention of the divine ox as the go-between, he and the Girl Weaver become husband and wife.

They live happily and prosperously for several years, during which a son and a daughter are born. In the meantime, the old ox dies, causing great grief in the family, and is buried like a father.

The Ethereal Emperor on high, on hearing about the misconduct of his granddaughter, is very angry that she, a deity, should have married a mortal and orders her, under pain of her family's destruction, to return right away to her weaving loom in Heaven.

For the lives of her dear ones, she has to comply meekly and starts flying back to her home in the sky. Cowherd, returning home from work to find his dear wife gone, picks up his wailing children. Carrying them in baskets, one attached to each end of a bamboo shoulder pole, he runs after her.

The Girl Weaver has to hurry on in spite of her own feelings, with Cowherd racing to catch up. This has gone on for some time when Xi Wangmu, Supreme Goddess in Paradise, happens to pass by. She points with her hairpin and a river appears in between the husband and wife, inter-

74

rupting the chase. Upon inquiring about their case, the Goddess gets the consent of the Emperor in Heaven to allow them to come together once a year on the seventh day of the seventh moon of the Chinese lunar calendar. And on that day, out of sympathy for the loving but distressed couple, birds of all descriptions come together to make a feathery bridge across the river (which is the Milky Way in the sky) so that they may walk across.

But on the other 300-odd days of the years, they (the stars Altair and Vega) have to remain separated by the Milky Way. Altair (Cowherd) has two small stars next to it, one on each side, and people say they are his two children in the baskets he is carrying on his shoulder-pole.

In China, when husbands live and work in places quite far from their wives, people would say these couples live a Cowherd-and-Girl-Weaver life. Now that you've read this brief tale, you know why.

NÜWA REPAIRS THE HEAVENS

女娲補天 *(Nüwa Bu Tian)*

This is a myth about the struggle of the ancient Chinese against Nature.

In remote ages, it says, the pillars which supported the vault of heaven along the four borders of the earth were broken, causing a cataclysm in the land of Shenzhou (as China was called). There were conflagrations in some parts and great floods in others. Wild animals ran rampant, playing havoc with the people. In this chaos emerged a great heroine by the name of Nüwa. She melted down stones of five colours to repair the vault of heaven, cut off the legs of the Great Tortoise to support the borders of the sky, put out the big fires, subdued the torrential floods and killed the fierce birds and beasts. The people once again lived in peace and happiness.

It is a beautiful myth which sings praise of Nüwa as courage and wisdom incarnate and embodies the aspirations of the ancient people to control the natural elements. That is why it has become a favourite subject for Chinese poets and artists.

Incidentally, according to another classical source, Nüwa is said to be the daughter of the Water Spirit, born three months after her brother Fuxi. Brother and sister were married and begot all of mankind. So, they are said to be the ancestors of the human race. Later, such marriages were forbidden and wedding customs and ceremonies were introduced, according to which men and women had to be of different parentage in order to marry. From this legend one can see the vestiges of ancient matriarchal society.

PANGU CREATES THE UNIVERSE

盤古開天闢地 *(Pangu Kai Tian Pi Di)*

Pangu, according to ancient Chinese mythology, was the creator of the universe. His Great Exploit first appeared in writing in a work of the Period of the Three Kingdoms about 3rd century A.D.

It is said that before the Great Beginning, the universe was like an egg and Pangu was formed inside, out of the two great principles *Yin* (feminine) and *Yang* (masculine). He underwent nine metamorphoses a day, affecting all around him. The clear and bright went up to become the sky, while the dirty and dark sank down to form the earth. The sky kept moving up, the earth becoming thicker and Pangu himself growing taller – all by ten feet a day. It went on like this for 18,000 years and the result was that the sky was immensely high, the earth immensely thick and Pangu himself immensely tall.

Another millennium passed, Pangu grew old and died. Different parts of his body disintegrated to become the sun, the moon, the stars, wind and cloud, mountain and river, land and field, grass and wood, metal and stone, in short all that we find in the visible universe.

Pangu, therefore, is the Hero of the Chinese Genesis, well known and liked by the people. He is usually taken as a subject by the painter or handicraftsman. His image, however, may be different according to the fancy of the artist: a dwarf dressed in animal skin or fig-leaves or a human figure with two horns on his head, carrying a hammer and a chisel.

CROSSROADS

三岔口 *(San Cha Kou)*

This is the title of a play one finds in all types of traditional opera productions in China. The story is simple and serves only as a flimsy excuse for the actors to exhibit their acrobatic skills. But as it is one of the pieces most readily understood and appreciated by foreign audiences, with little dialogue and less singing, it is often included in the repertoire of a Chinese dramatic company touring abroad. So it deserves a brief synopsis.

Jiao Zan, a loyal Song dynasty military officer falling victim to a political intrigue, is being exiled under escort. His friend Ren Tanghui, fearing that he might meet with some misadventure on the way, shadows him and the guards to afford him secret protection. After Jiao Zan enters an inn at a fork in the road, the friend follows.

The innkeeper Liu Lihua, a man trained in martial arts and an admirer of Jiao, finds Ren's behavior extraordinary, like that of a would-be assassin. Ren, on his part, also finds the innkeeper's manner indescribably unusual.

At night, Liu steals into the room of Ren who, instead of sleeping, is all keyed up and on his guard. (At this moment, the fully-illuminated stage must be assumed to be in total darkness.) The two grope around in the dark, each trying to get at the other. They come within an inch of each other but fail to see anything. Fists are struck out but miss by a hair; shining swords are swished about at random, to be inadvertently dodged in the last split-second.

This scene, which lasts about fifteen minutes, is the body of the one-act play; it is a breath-taking fifteen minutes, punctuated with laughter-provoking close shaves.

Finally the din of the fighting wakes up Jiao Zan, who comes in, followed by Liu's wife with a candle light. The misunderstanding is cleared.

A DIVINE MAIDEN
SCATTERS FLOWERS

天女散花 *(Tian Nü San Hua)*

This story originates from the Buddhist scriptures. According to *The Sutra of Vimalakirti**, in the hall of this great master there was an ethereal maiden (*devi* in Sankrit, meaning a female *deva*), who scattered divine flowers. The flowers would fall off the Bodhisattvas, but they would stick on the chief disciple, showing that he still had a long way to go before the attainment of supreme wisdom. The devi said of him, "the flowers do not fall off his person because his deep-rooted habits are not yet fully eliminated."

Later Chinese writers and story-tellers gave a twist to the original religious message of this simple Buddhist tale and *Tian Nü San Hua* came to mean that when spring comes divine maidens will scatter flowers from on high to embellish the human world.

Works of art created on this theme strive to convey the feeling of renewed vitality and exuberant beauty.

---

* Vimalakirti was a contemporary of Sakyamuni (Gautama Buddha). A lay Buddhist, he was famous for his great eloquence in expounding the doctrines of the Mahayana (Great Vehicle) School.

PRINCESS WENCHENG
文成公主 *(Wencheng Gongzhu)*

There are two well-known monasteries in Lhasa which are historically connected with Princess Wencheng (?-600 A.D.) of the Tang dynasty. One, the Ramogia Monastery, was built by her, and the other, the Jokhan Monastery, has down to this day a beautiful statue built by the Tibetans to honour her memory.

An adopted daughter of the outstanding Tang Emperor Tai Zong (599-649 A.D.), she was married by the emperor to Songtsan Gambo (? 617-650), ruler of the Tubo, forefathers of the Tibetans, in the year 641 A.D.

A modern drama in Tang costume written by the late playwright Tian Han is still being repeatedly staged, telling about her trip to Tibet and her marriage to the ruler in spite of obstructive forces working against it in the courts of both sides.

The special envoy sent by the Tibetan ruler to press his suit at Chang'an (present-day Xi'an) had to go through various difficult tests before the emperor could give his consent to the proposal. He acquitted himself brilliantly in several tests during almost a year's stay at the Tang capital. His followers, especially the deputy envoy, had exhausted their patience, when the last and most difficult test of all was set: the envoy was to single out the princess, whom he had never met, from a pageant of some thousand identically-dressed young maidens.

The evening before the event, an elderly matron of the hostel, who had waited on the princess over a period of years, called on the envoy and acquainted him with her particular facial characteristics. When the envoy thanked her, she said that he had only the Tang emperor himself to be thankful to. It appeared that His Majesty, with the foresight of a great statesman, had already made up his mind about the Tang-Tibet union.

Before Princess Wencheng began her long journey, a report came to the knowledge of the emperor alleging that Songtsan

Gambo was an old man over seventy, while the bride-to-be was not quite twenty.

Meanwhile, individual courtiers were for conquering Tibet by force of arms instead of cementing relations with it through inter-marriage between the reigning houses.

The Tang emperor soon established the Tibetan monarch as a young man in his middle 20's and convinced his warlike ministers of the desirability of peaceful relations with the border people.

The objection to this wedlock from the Tang courtiers, however, was not as serious, nor as underhanded, as that from a clique of bigwigs close to the Tibetan ruler.

The deputy envoy sent to Chang'an was one of the handful. The task of accompanying the bridal party back to Tibet fell on him since the chief envoy had been asked by the Tang emperor to stay on as his counsellor on Tibetan affairs. On the way, he kept sending secret reports to Lhasa bringing trumped-up charges of various "misdeeds" against the princess. Furthermore, conniving with his father in Lhasa, he tampered with the message from Gambo to his future queen and spirited off the messenger.

Gambo's message was that he would leave Lhasa and come up north to welcome the princess at the relatively delightful grassland of Yushu. This was distorted to read that the princess' party should move their camp and wait in a desolate area north of the torrential Nujiang River, a suggestion which she followed with great reluctance. So when Gambo arrived at Yushu, he was disappointed to find the princess gone. This created the impression that each side was slighting or trying to dodge the other. The hardships experienced by the princess' party, what with moving, interminable waiting, inclement weather and shortage of supplies, were particularly harsh; there was talk of turning back to Chang'an, which would amount to a virtual breakoff of the betrothal.

Patience and better judgement, nevertheless, prevailed over

suspicions. A skeptical Songtsan Gambo came to join the waiting princess and happened upon her just in time to save her from the jaws of a tiger while she was out sight-seeing. Each pretended to be somebody else but could not help secretly admiring the other.

Finally the plot was unraveled and the culprits caught. And a grand wedding ceremony in the Potala Palace marks the end of the play.

History records the progress made under the influence of the princess and that of Songtsan Gambo, who was himself an admirer of the Tang culture. Many of the achievements of the Han people, including various farming methods, the grindstone, handicrafts, pottery, paper-making, sericulture, wine-brewing, the Han calendar and Chinese medicine were introduced into Tibet. All these gave a fillip to the economic and cultural development of the Tubo and helped to forge closer links between the Han and the Tibetan nationalities.

For this reason, Princess Wencheng is remembered as one who made indelible contributions to the solidarity of China as a multinational country and, in Tibet itself, she is revered even today as a demigoddess.

CAI WENJI RETURNS TO THE HAN
文姬歸漢 *(Wenji Gui Han)*

The Story of Cai Wenji, a celebrated poetess and woman scholar living at the end of the Han dynasty (in the 3rd century A.D.), is that of Princess Wencheng and Wang Zhaojun in reverse (see articles *Wencheng Gongzhu* and *Zhaojun Chu Sai*). Unlike the latter who leave their homeland to be married to the rulers of border peoples, she returns to China proper after she has been the wife of a Xiongnu (Hun) prince.

The only daughter of Cai Yong, famous scholar-official who died in prison as a victim of rivalries over power, she herself was noted for her attainments in literature, historical studies, poetry and music.

During the chaotic fighting among the various political and military factions, people had to abandon their homes. Eighteen-year old Wenji, fleeing for safety with an aunt, was captured by undisciplined troops but was rescued by a Xiongnu prince who brought her back to his country and made her his consort.

During twelve years of sojourn in the land of the Xiongnu, she bore the prince a son and a daughter.

A well-known play written by the late Guo Moruo (Kuo Mo-jo) under the title *Cai Wenji* begins with a special mission sent by Cao Cao, Prime Minister of the Han, to the king of the Huns with precious gifts to negotiate for her return to China. Cao Cao wanted her to carry on with her late father's unfinished work *Sequel to the Chronicles of the Han*.

The mission nearly resulted in failure because Zhou Jin, deputy head of the delegation, tried to bluff the Xiongnu into agreement with a show of armed strength. The prince was not one to swallow a threat, and Wenji herself, out of her desire to see lasting friendship between the two peoples, would not agree to go back to the Han under military duress.

However, it happened that Dong Si, head of the mission, was a cousin of Wenji's. During a conversation between the two (which Wenji arranged to let the prince overhear), Dong Si assured her that there were no troops following up, that

Prime Minister Cao Cao wished only to befriend the northern neighbours and that the purpose in bringing her back was to enable her to enrich the cultural life of the country. Upon hearing this, the prince came into the yurt. Not only did he agree that Wenji should return, but he struck an immediate friendship with Dong Si, exchanging swords and court regalia with Dong after the Xiongnu custom.

The prince, nevertheless, would not agree to let the children go. Wenji was torn between conflicting emotions—eagerness to go home and sadness at parting with her children. To ease matters, her aunt, out of her own choice, stayed behind to bring them up.

On the long trek back through the northern wilderness, she wrote her famous *Eighteen Laments on the Hujia** to give vent to her feelings. And passing near her father's tomb, she ordered the entourage to pitch camp and spent a sleepless night there chanting her poignant lines. Dong Si had to come out of his tent to console her and persuade her to place the great task that had fallen to her above her personal sorrows.

An injury caused by a fall from his horse prevented Dong Si from reaching Yexia (the provisional capital, in today's Hebei province) with the party. Cao Cao, misled by an insinuating report from Zhou Jin to conclude that Dong Si had had illicit relations with Wenji and particularly with the Xiongnu prince, issued an order for Dong Si to commit suicide. But thanks to Wenji's defence and explanations, backed by the testimony of the waiting maids who had been present on the occasions in question, he commended Dong Si on the brilliant discharge of his duties as an envoy and promoted him.

For eight years, Wenji sorted out and edited her father's manuscripts on Han history. Her children, following the death of their father, were sent back to her. At the prompt-

---

* *Hujia*, a reed musical instrument of the northern tribes.

ing of Cao Cao, she was remarried to Dong Si, the man who had brought her back and whose life she had saved.

THE WESTERN QUEEN MOTHER

西王母 *(Xi Wangmu)*

Mythical stories about this deity appear in quite a number of ancient works in which she is called by different names — Xi Wangmu, Jin Mu (Golden Mother), Xi Lao (Western Granny) or, most popular among the people, Wangmu Niangniang (Lady Queen Mother) — and described variously, ranging from a monster with a leopard's tail and tiger's teeth to a thirty-year-old goddess of rare beauty.

One of the stories gives her a husband, Dong Wanggong, with whom she meets once a year. The two are supposed to be the Supreme Divine Beings in the world of the gods and their union engendered the heavens and the earth and everything in the universe.

Generally, however, she appears alone in most of the myths as a gorgeously-dressed Supreme Goddess, graceful in bearing and gracious in manner. She lives on top of the snow-clad Western Kunlun Mountains in palaces of gold and jade, surrounded by fabulous flower-gardens and orchards bearing "peaches of immortality". Her palace is flanked by Jasper Lake on the left and encircled by the Emerald River on the right.

On the third day of the third moon every year (others say every 3,000 years), when the peaches ripen, she holds a grand birthday banquet to which she invites all the deities and divinities to partake of the peaches which have the mystic virtue of bestowing immortality on whoever eats them.

According to written literature of different sources, she has helped several virtuous emperors and leaders to conquer their enemies, improve the administration of their country or to come to know the Way of Illumination.

Popular theatre in later ages, however, presents her as an elderly lady with the appearance of a sort of Dowager Empress. But like all deities created by man, she is sometimes "written down". For instance, in *Da Nao Tiangong* (Cf. article under that title), together with all the hierarchy in Heaven, she is even turned into a butt of mild mockery.

Incidentally, Jasper Lake (*Yaochi* in Chinese) by which she lives has become a synonym for Paradise, and *jia fan Yaochi* (meaning "her carriage has returned to Jasper Lake"), an euphemism for an elderly lady's death.

THE WESTERN CHAMBER

西廂記 *(Xi Xiang Ji)*

One of the most frequently enacted plays over a long historical period, *The Western Chamber,* is still very much seen on the stage today and is widely used in other forms of art. It was first written as an opera by Wang Shifu of the Yuan Dynasty towards the end of the 13th century on the basis of a much earlier Tang Dynasty tale.

The romance takes place in a monastery from beginning to end.

Zhang Gong, a young scholar who was travelling around the country, met Yingying when he was visiting the Pujiu Monastery. Struck by her beauty, he found out on inquiry that she was the daughter of the late Prime Minister and, because of troubled times, was temporarily staying with her mother Madame Cui in the western chamber of the monastery; when the situation improved, they would continue their journey home with her father's coffin.

Upon meeting Hong Niang (Maid Rose), Yingying's clever young handmaid, Zhang introduced himself, giving his name, native place, age as well as his bachelor status all in one breath. Hong Niang took him to be a fool and later told her young mistress about it.

Zhang overheard Yingying's evening prayers in the garden and divined that she on her part was favourably impressed with him, too.

All of a sudden, the monastery was surrounded by insurrectionary troops led by an officer named Sun the Flying Tiger, who made it known that his sole intention was to make Yingying his wife and mistress of his camp.

Panic-stricken, Madame Cui had it proclaimed in the prayer hall to a gathering of the monks and the laity that whoever could induce the rebel host to retire would get Yingying as his bride with a handsome dowry.

Out came the young scholar Zhang Gong with a suggestion, which was readily accepted and put into execution. Yingying was promised to Sun the Flying Tiger but the wedding could only take place three days later after a religious ceremony which would absolve her from the mourning rites for her father. In the meantime, Zhang wrote a letter to his friend General Du Que, Commander of an army guarding a nearby pass, asking him to come speedily to his rescue. The letter was delivered by a brave monk in the kitchen, who fought his way through the siege.

As soon as General Du arrived with his troops, the rebels surrendered. Thereupon, Madame Cui thanked Zhang for his help and invited him to dinner the next day.

At the dinner, however, the old lady went back on her word. She repeatedly encouraged Yingying to serve Zhang drinks as her "elder brother", then informed Zhang that during the lifetime of the Prime Minister Yingying had already been betrothed to a nephew of hers.

Zhang's heart-breaking disappointment won the sympathy of Hong Niang, who promised to help. She acted as a willing messenger in the exchange of love poems, and often enlivened the gloomy longings of the young couple with her well-intended teasing.

At last, a poem Hong Niang brought from Yingying to Zhang Gong read as follows:

I wait for the moonlight at the western chamber,
To shine through my door left ajar.
May my beloved one be not afar
And miss flower-shadows on the wall astir.

At this thinly-disguised invitation, Zhang Gong arrived at the young girl's chamber in the evening, only to be chided gently by Yingying and mocked by Hong Niang.

He fell ill of lovesickness. And Hong Niang was sent again with a poem from Yingying to console him. This was followed by a personal visit by the fair lady accompanied by Hong Niang to dispel her shyness.

Before long, as these nightly assignations became more frequent, the old lady noticed something unusual and put the maid Hong Niang in the dock. At first she denied anything had happened; after a beating, she put the blame on Madame Cui for her breach of promise. Furthermore, she cleverly argued, what had happened could not be undone and to bring the matter before the authorities would only disgrace the family. This brought her mistress round.

Zhang Gong was called over and promised the hand of Yingying provided that he succeeded in his candidacy at the forthcoming imperial examinations. He was to proceed to the capital the very next day.

The play ends with a tearful farewell feast for Zhang Gong and his dream of a happy reunion with Yingying on his first night at an inn after setting out. The audience is left in suspense.

The character Hong Niang is so much liked that some modern dramatists have rewritten the play to give her the prominence over Yingying. Her role is naturally played by the prima donna and the title of the piece is changed into *Hong Niang*.

In everyday language, when somebody is called a Hong Niang, it means that he or she will help, or has helped, a pair of lovers come together by acting as go-between or match-maker.

THE SPIRIT OF RIVER XIANG AND THE NYMPH OF RIVER HAN

湘君·湘夫人 *(Xiang Jun, Xiang Furen)*

These are two mythical figures first mentioned in the *Nine Odes* believed to have been rewritten on the basis of popular songs by Qu Yuan, a great poet who lived some time near the beginning of the 3rd century B.C. But there have been two or three different interpretations as to their exact identity.

One interpretation says that they were the two wives of the legendary Emperor Shun, by the name of E'huang and Nüying. When news reached them that Shun had died abroad during an inspection tour, they rushed south to Dongting Lake (in present-day Hunan province). Tears running dry, they drowned themselves in the River Xiang, and were transformed into two nymphs called Xiang Jun and Xiang Furen.

Another version says simply that Xiang Jun (Lord Xiang) is the male spirit of the River Xiang (in Hunan), who married the nymph of the River Han (in Hubei). As his wife, she became known as Xiang Furen (Lady Xiang).

The consensus of opinion is generally inclined to the second interpretation.

The original poem is a touching description of the trip made by Xiang Jun to the north to court the water nymph and of her longing for him. It also sings of a fantasy Xiang Jun had about building an under-water mansion in which to live with his sweetheart and receiving the congratulatory visits of other spirits. In short, it is a love poem couched in a mythical tale.

Ivory carvings made on this theme show Xiang Jun sailing north on a "flying dragon" over rippling waters and Xiang Furen, on board of a cassia barge, coming to meet him.

A YOUNG BEAUTY WHO AVENGES HER COUNTRY

西施 *(Xishi)*

A famous heroine of the Spring and Autumn Period, Xishi was, according to some accounts, originally a country girl of matchless beauty who washed silk for a living in Zhuji of the state of Yue (roughly present-day Zhejiang province).

It was about the middle of the 5th century B.C. Yue was vanquished by the neighbouring state of Wu (roughly Jiangsu province). Goujian, the Prince of Yue, taken prisoner, had to serve Fuchai, Prince of Wu, for three years in the most humiliating manner before he was released.

Back in his own country, he resolved to seek vengeance. For fear that he might forget his humiliation, he eschewed the comforts of the palace. He slept on brushwood and outside his hut hung a bladder of gall, which he tasted before each meal, to remind himself of the bitterness he had gone through.

Apart from various measures taken for national rehabilitation, he ordered his ministers to look for beautiful maidens to be presented as tribute to Prince Fuchai. It was Fan Li who discovered Xishi, while she was washing silk yarn by a stream. She was not only beautiful but also sensible, intelligent and ready to sacrifice herself to avenge her prince and her country. She was brought to the state of Wu.

Scarcely had Xishi arrived there when Fuchai became enamoured of her, taking her as a fairy maiden who had descended from Heaven. From then on, in such a fair company, the Prince of Wu abandoned himself to a life of worldly pleasures, if not downright debauchery, and neglected the administration of his country. He even consulted his new favourite concubine on important state affairs, with results always to the advantage of her own country. She was also instrumental in the death by suicide, ordered by Prince Fuchai, of the country's Commander-in-Chief. The state of Wu declined in strength and prosperity.

In the meantime, Yue grew rich and strong.

In the next war between the two feuding states, Yue

delivered Wu a resounding defeat but, in view of its remnant strength, concluded a peace on favourable terms. Nine years later, however, Yue completely wiped out and annexed Wu. Prince Fuchai committed suicide.

There are different versions as to the end of Xishi after having served her country in such a unique manner. One account says that she vanished, no one knows where. Another claims that she drowned herself. A third alleges that she sailed away with Fan Li, the minister who discovered her.

Xishi is also known as Xizi and has been associated with West Lake ("Xihu" in Chinese, also called "Xizi Lake") of Hangzhou, not only because this lake is in her native land but because, in comparing the beauty of both, Su Dongpo, the Song dynasty poet, wrote these famous lines:

To Xizi the Lake is to be compared,
Equally charming, in heavy make-up or light.

Perhaps it would not be out of place to add here that Fan Li is also a well-known historical figure. After serving Prince Goujian of Yue faithfully throughout years of hardship, he abruptly cut short his official career at the height of his success by eloping, let's suppose, with Xishi. It is said that he went into business under the pseudonym "Duke of Taozhu" and, amassing great wealth in a few years' time, became the first Chinese millionaire. In the old days, he was considered a patron saint by Chinese businessmen.

Knowing the caprices of kings and princes, he left a colleague the following epigram before abandoning his official position: "When game birds are finished, the fine bow will be shelved; when the cunning hares are all dead, the running dog (hound) will be cooked." His friend did not heed his advice and was eventually forced to commit suicide by Prince Goujian whom he had served meritoriously.

The expression "running dog" which, it is believed, found its way into the English language via Chinese, came originally from Fan Li of the 5th century B.C.

A MOTHER TATTOOS HER SON

岳母刺字 *(Yue Mu Ci Zi)*

There is a temple northwest of the West Lake in Hangzhou dedicated to the memory of Yue Fei, one of the greatest, and also one of the most tragic, national heroes in the history of China.

Yue Fei (1103-1142 A.D.) started his military career as a junior officer towards the end of the Northern Song Dynasty. He was expelled from military service because of a petition he wrote to the Emperor Gao Zong advising against moving the capital to the south under the pressure of an advancing northern tribe.

Soon his talents came to be appreciated by General Zong Ze, who employed him as a senior officer in his troops guarding Kaifeng. After Zong's death, he moved south with the army, now under Du Chong's command.

In the year 1129 the northern invaders led by Wuzhu of the Jin Dynasty (Golden Tartars) crossed the Yangtse River in a bid to occupy all of China. It was Yue Fei who put up a strong resistance and, with the help of the people, forced the enemy to withdraw back to the north of the river. In the course of the zig-zag, Nanjing was recovered.

This was followed by other victories, culminating in a resounding defeat he administered to Wuzhu's hordes in Henan in 1135, as a result of which important cities like Zhengzhou and Luoyang were relieved from enemy occupation. In the meantime, he was promoted to be a satrap. His successes greatly encouraged the local people, who organized themselves into many volunteer units and rose against the Jin invaders.

Yue Fei's efforts to recover all lost lands, however, were not supported by the capitulationist court. The Emperor Gao Zong and the Prime Minister Qin Hui were both for peace at any price. Yue doggedly resisted this tendency, but in vain. He was summoned back to the southern capital (now, the tourist city of Hangzhou) and stripped of all military power. This was followed by a false accusation of treason, and he was thrown into gaol.

On January 27, 1143 (29th day of the 12th moon of 1142 by the lunar calendar), he was put to death under a charge which, in the words of his persecutors, "does not have to be there". He was only thirty-nine. Executed at the same time were his adopted son Yue Yun and a faithful follower Zhang Xian, both patriotic warriors. Yue Fei was secretly buried by an admiring gaol guard who stole his remains from the execution site at the risk of his life.

He was posthumously rehabilitated by later emperors to allay mounting public indignation. In the year 1163 under the reign of Xiao Zong, that is, some 20 years after his death, he was re-buried with appropriate rites where his tomb now is, by the side of the temple and, in the reign of Emperor Ning Zong (1195-1224), the honorific title of Prince Yue was bestowed on him.

The Chinese people remember him as the hero who rallied his countrymen to fight back as they were being forced to retreat under the hoofs of the nomadic invaders. Yue Fei's exploits have gone through artistic re-creation to become operas, plays, works of fiction or tales told by story-tellers. Often they are illustrated in decorations of valuable furniture and porcelain. His name continues to shine in the hearts of the Chinese people, especially in times of foreign menace.

A four-character horizontal inscription in Chinese, "Return Our Rivers and Mountains", copied in his bold and elegant handwriting, often adorn the office walls of military officers and statesmen.

His patriotism is at least partly attributed to the education he received from a judicious mother. Having lost his father at an early age, he was brought up by his widowed mother, who constantly reminded him of the perils faced by the country.

A Peking Opera play under the same title as this article tells how he was disappointed with the leadership of Du Chong

107

(see above), the new commander of the army in which he served as a senior officer. The man besides being cruel and wilful, would not listen to his counsel as to how to administer the troops and conduct warfare. He came home on leave, intending to resign from his post and remain at home to fulfil his filial duties. Upon hearing this, the mother voiced her disagreement, remonstrating with him that he should subordinate personal grievances to the great cause of defending the country and recovering lost territory. He accepted his mother's criticism. And for fear that he might forget, his mother personally tattooed four Chinese characters on his back — *"Jing Zhong Bao Guo"*, meaning "Serve the Motherland in Ardent Loyalty".

He returned to the barracks the next day with renewed resolve.

AN EMPEROR'S SON-IN-LAW PUT TO THE CHOPPER

鍘美案 *(Zha Mei An)*
or 秦香蓮 *(Qin Xianglian)*

Qin Xianglian, a woman in her early middle age, came to the capital Kaifeng (Henan province) with her young son and daughter, looking for her husband Chen Shimei.

They had been married about 10 years when Chen bade a tearful good-bye to his parents, wife and children and left for the capital about a thousand leagues away to sit for the imperial examination. That was three years before. Since then, nothing had been heard from him. But famine struck in the meantime; the old couple died of illness and starvation, while Xianglian and the children were forced by circumstances to go out in search of Chen.

It was not difficult to learn of Chen Shimei's whereabouts in Kaifeng. For he had won the first place of honour in the examinations and had married one of the emperor's daughters.

At the palace of the imperial son-in-law, Xianglian was barred from entrance. Chen Shimei refused to see her. That is, not until she had won the sympathy of the guard and rushed inside. Chen still pretended not to know her, for fear that this would implicate him in the grave offence of having deceived the sovereign about his marital status and thus jeopardise his prestigious position and happy future. The wife's pleas and the children's tears all failed to move his hardened heart.

Roaming the streets of the capital, Xianglian appealed to a passing elderly courtier and convinced him of her sad story. The latter invited Chen Shimei to a party at which Xianglian, playing the part of a wandering woman bard, was made to sing her own story. This and the host's expostulations served only to enrage the adamant husband, who left the party abruptly.

Furthermore, he ordered one of his followers by the name of Han Qi to go to the temple where Xianglian and the children were taking shelter and assassinate them all. Han Qi, however, upon hearing Xianglian's tragic experience, was filled with sympathy and could not bring himself to carry

110

out the order. Instead he told them to flee for their lives, while he himself committed suicide. His sword, bearing the heraldry of the imperial son-in-law's palace, fell into Xianglian's hands, later to be used as evidence against Chen.

With all her hopes shattered, Xianglian was driven to desperation. Filled with hatred, she sued her husband at the Court of the Lord Governor Bao Zheng for desertion and attempted murder. Now Bao was famous for his impartial and incorruptible character, and the heinous crimes of the emperor's son-in-law filled him with righteous indignation.

He invited Chen over to his palace for a meeting and, after failing to persuade him to make amends, had him arrested and tried.

The news alarmed the empress and her daughter, Chen's second wife. They came personally to the Governor's court to intervene on Chen's behalf. This threw the Governor into a quandary, much as he wanted to avenge Xianglian for the wrongs she had suffered. He offered her three hundred taels of silver to terminate the case, with the advice that she should leave the scene, bring up the children but ask them never to become officials.

Xianglian sighed, "In spite of all I have heard about the Lord Governor, he is no exception to the rule that bureaucrats shield one another." Whereupon, Bao Zheng, taking off his official hat to show his determination come what might, ordered Chen Shimei, son-in-law of the emperor himself, to be executed.

The above is one of a series of tales about Bao Zheng (999-1062), a historical figure who lived under the Northern Song. As an official, he was noted for his courage, his upright and indomitable character and, to borrow a Chinese expression, his "iron-faced disinterestedness". That is why, in Peking Opera, the actor playing the part of this character usually has his face painted almost completely black.

The historical Bao Zheng, in his official career, rose up to a post similar to today's Vice-Minister of Defence and for some time was Lord Governor of Greater Kaifeng. It was in the latter post that he showed his mettle as an astute, upright and courageous judge defending always the interests of the innocent in spite of the pressures of nepotism, wealth and power. He has been so very much admired by people down to this day, that he is still popularly referred to by the reverent title of "Bao Gong" (Lord Bao).

The cases tried by him went through a process of romantic exaggeration in later years and, together with some pure inventions, grew into scores of thrice re-told tales. These eventually found their way into popular Chinese fiction, drama and, to a lesser degree, other realms of art.

ZHAOJUN GOES BEYOND THE GREAT WALL

昭君出塞 *(Zhaojun Chu Sai)*

This is the story of Wang Zhaojun, a maid in the palace of Emperor Yuan (48-33 B.C.) of the Western Han dynasty. It tells how she was married off to a *chanyu* (king) of the Xiongnu (Huns).

A beautiful girl of Zigui county in western Hubei province, she was selected to become a maid of honour in the imperial palace. There she found herself one among many rivals, few of whom would have any opportunity to find favour with the emperor. The practice then was for the official painter, whose name was Mao Yanshou, to paint the maids' portraits. On the basis of these, the sovereign made his choice of consorts. It was also the practice for the palace maids to bribe the painter to prettify their portraits. Zhaojun, however, assured of her own beauty, would not stoop to such sordid measures. So no portrait was ever made of her and, consequently, the presence of such a rare beauty in the palace never came to the attention of the ruler.

Emperor Yuan, seeking to neutralize a nomadic tribe in the northern desert, decided to marry off one of the palace maids to a friendly king of the Huns. This time, one of the homely ones would be chosen, although the title of "Princess" was to be bestowed on her. Mao Yanshou the painter, bearing a grudge against Zhaojun, produced a distorted portrait of her and presented it to the emperor. This resulted in her being chosen as the future queen of a nomadic people roaming the deserts of the far north.

It was not until the time of Zhaojun's departure that the emperor, seeing her for the first time, was struck by her seraphic beauty and tranquil grace. It was too late! Furious, he had Mao Yanshou beheaded, while the tearful bride-to-be, full of remorse, embarked on a long trek north outside the Great Wall.

Various types of opera have presented this tragic piece under the title *Zhaojun Chu Sai*, which was based on the above traditional legend.

Traditional works of art and literature depicted Zhaojun as a victim of corrupt officialdom. Modern historical research, however, throws a different light on the episode.

In the year 33 B.C., Huhanye, a king of the Huns who was friendly toward the people of the interior, came on a personal visit to the Han capital of Chang'an (present-day Xi'an). By way of cementing amicable relations, he asked the Han ruler for a wife. The emperor had this proclaimed in his harem, and called for a volunteer, promising to make her a princess if she would be willing to marry the head of a border people.

Now the maids of honour in the palace were like canaries in a golden cage, left often to pine away and die unnoticed. Few of them ever had the opportunity to leave the quarters to which they were confined. They longed for freedom and for marriage, even to the lowest in station among the common people. But at the mention of a nomadic tribe − a people considered to be semi-barbarians at that time, who would want to take up such a challenge?

Zhaojun, however, an intelligent girl fully aware of the significance of this union, volunteered. The northern king was greatly impressed by her beauty. Eventually she won the love and respect of the Hun people also. This inter-marriage brought sixty years of peace on China's northern frontier.

A modern drama was written in the light of this interpretation and became an immediate hit on the Beijing stage. The play, touching on the desolate and hopeless life of the palace girls, deals mainly with the patient, painstaking efforts which Zhaojun made in the face of adverse forces after she began her life among the Huns and which finally won her the love and confidence of her once-skeptical husband and his people.

ZHONG KUI

鍾馗打鬼 *(Zhong Kui Da Gui)*

You probably will meet him in a shop dealing in old paintings. There he is, an ugly, fiendish-looking man, with glowering eyes and bristling beard, usually perched on one leg brandishing a sword — painted on a scroll.

Just as the ancient beauties provide the artist with scope for painting what is extremely beautiful, Zhong Kui gives him an opportunity to revel with his paint-brush in what is ferocious and grotesque.

A legendary figure first mentioned in a Song dynasty book, Zhong was supposed to have lived under the Tang during the reign of the Emperor Xuan Zong.

Once the emperor fell ill and failed for months to respond to treatment.

One night he had a dream in which he saw two ghosts. One was small in stature, clad in red, with one foot bare, holding a large paper fan. The spirit, it seemed, wanted to steal the emperor's jade flute and the musk bag of the favourite imperial concubine Yang Guifei. Jumping and circling the palatial hall, he was chased by another ghost of great height and powerful build. The latter wore a hat and blue clothes, with one arm exposed and both feet bare. He seized hold of the small one, gouged out both of his eyes, split him into two and ate him up.

Astounded, the emperor asked him who he was. The big ghost replied, "Zhong Kui is the name. I died after failing in the imperial examination for military officers. I have, anyway, long resolved to wipe out all demons and monsters. So I am at it now."

As soon as he woke up, the emperor felt well again. Wu Daozi the famous painter was summoned for an imperial audience and told about the dream. By imperial order, he set about painting Zhong Kui's portrait according to the emperor's description. The result was the exact likeness of the ghost seen in the dream.

For the later generations, therefore, Zhong Kui became an

117

idol thought to be capable of eliminating ghosts and demons, and as mentioned above, he also became one of the favourite themes for painters. In the old days, people used to nang his portrait up in their homes on the Dragon Boat Festival (the fifth day of the fifth lunar month) to keep off evil spirits.

ZHUO WENJUN

卓文君 *(Zhuo Wenjun)*

According to a work of the fourth century, Zhuo Wenjun was a girl who lived under the Western Han dynasty. Daughter of a rich nobleman of Linqiong (now Ya'an) of Sichuan, she was not only exceedingly beautiful but widely read and well versed in music. Her fate as a widow at the tender age of seventeen seemed to promise only long tedious years of loneliness, but she was by nature unconventional and romantic.

Sima Xiangru, renowned at the time and in posterity as a great prose-poet, paid her father a visit. Seeing her, he was attracted by her good looks, and played on the zither to press his courtship. And during the night she secretly went to join him at his residence. They unbosomed to each other their mutual admiration and tasted the ecstasies of love.

Then they eloped to Chengdu, where they began to experience the hardships of poverty and were vexed by mundane necessities. To dispel Wenjun's depression, Xiangru took off his precious bird's-feather gown and exchanged it for wine. Wenjun who was used to the luxuries of wealth was moved to tears.

They thought out a scheme and opened up a shop and began to sell wine for a living, with Wenjun tending the stove and Xiangru washing the dishes, in order to bring shame on her rich but unsympathetic father.

Sensitive to this loss of face, the father gave her rich donations, and Wenjun became wealthy again. And the couple grew even more devoted to each other.

Years later, however, Xiangru took fancy to another girl, intending to take her as concubine. Wenjun satirized the idea and pleaded with him in a poem entitled *The Song of Hoary Heads*. Deeply touched, he gave up the idea.

After Xiangru's death, Wenjun wrote an elegy in mourning, a well-known piece of work appreciated by later generations.

Zhuo Wenjun is remembered as an image of beauty and talent, and as one of the earliest girls to fight for free choice in love. *Wenjun Listens to the Zither (Wenjun Ting Qin)* and *Wenjun Tends the Stove (Wenjun Dang Lu)* are celebrated scenes from the story of this daring, irrepressible woman true to her own passion.

SCENES FROM A DREAM OF RED MANSIONS

紅樓夢 *(Hong Lou Meng)*

Written in the eighteenth century largely by Cao Xueqin and completed by Gao E, *A Dream of Red Mansions (Hong Lou Meng,* also translated as *The Dream of the Red Chamber)* is a monument in literature and represents the peak of classical Chinese fiction.

No other romance has drawn so many scholars during the past two centuries to devote themselves to its research, nor has any other novel occasioned so much controversy, and so intense at times, as to its message, its significance, even its authorship. For the purpose of this book, however, suffice it to say that it is generally considered to be a political-historical novel tolling the knell of the landlord-aristocrat class and extolling the virtues as well as lamenting the plight of some young people, as represented by Jia Baoyu and Lin Daiyu, who put up a futile fight as rebels against this class that begot them and that had so much to give them of what they wanted so little.

This forceful saga of the Jia family unfolds itself around the tragic love of Baoyu and Daiyu and presents a panoramic genre-painting, a whole gallery of highly individual yet typical characters. Interwoven with the principal tragedy are a number of episodes involving secondary characters, each of which could be made into a full-fledged novelette. Yet, all these, through the ingenuity and artistry of the author, are well knit into a many-splendoured whole.

For this reason, it has provided, during the past 200 years, ample subject matter to the performing, graphic and plastic arts. And it is from this angle that a synopsis of the main story and certain scenes from the novel are described in the following pages.

BAOYU AND DAIYU

寶玉與黛玉 *(Baoyu yu Daiyu)*

Jia Baoyu is the favourite grandson of the old Lady Dowager and centre of attention in the princely mansion of the Jias.

A sensitive boy, he is disillusioned by the falsehood and vulgarity that he finds in his surroundings and grows boldly skeptical of certain aspects of feudal society. Thoroughly disgusted with the writing of stereotyped essays and the study of the classics as a preparation for the imperial examinations, he is drawn by poetry and literature as an art as well as the company of the girls around him.

Baoyu finds consolation in his young cousin Lin Daiyu when the latter, with the untimely death of her parents, settles down to live in the same mansion under the aegis of the same grandmother.

Daiyu is a girl as intelligent in mind as she is physically delicate. Living under the roof of relatives, most of whom are affected with hypocricy and snobbery, she feels disappointed and melancholy, a solitary flower in love with its own fragrance.

A common oppression, undefined as it is, draws Baoyu and Daiyu together and a true love springs up between them before they know it.

In the meantime, another female cousin of a maternal aunt of Baoyu's also moves into the mansion. Xue Baochai is from a rich family. Brought up according to the standards set in those days, she is outwardly gentle and sincere but inwardly egoistic and calculating. A staunch supporter of feudalism, she counsels Baoyu to study hard for an official career and, through artful fawning and suaveness, works her way into the favour of Baoyu's mother and grandmother, the Lady Dowager. And unlike Daiyu, she cultivates and enjoys smooth relations with all those around her.

The story unfolds not through melodramatics or coincidences, as in most of the novels before, but through everyday occurrences. Another important character is Wang Xifeng, wife of an older first cousin of Baoyu's, a capable young woman, as sinister as she is pretty, who wields real power in the grand household. By her scheming, a wedding is arranged during Baoyu's illness between him and the slick Baochai, but to enlist his cooperation he is told that the bride will be Daiyu. Meanwhile the latter is actually pining away with a broken heart.

On his wedding day, discovering that the bride is not the girl of his heart, Baoyu goes almost mad with disappointment, while Daiyu in her own chamber breathes her last amidst the distant sound of wedding music. The bridegroom, after crying his heart out over the loss of his sweetheart, departs for good from the palatial mansion to become a priest, leaving Baochai his wife in name only.

GRAND VIEW GARDEN
大觀園 *(Da Guan Yuan)*

This is the beautiful setting in which most of the events of the novel *Hong Lou Meng* take place.

Baoyu's father Jia Zheng, a typical orthodox official and one of the masters of the noble household, had an elder daughter Yuanchun, who was selected to enter the palace and later promoted to be a consort of the emperor. In this way, the Jias came to enjoy greater imperial grace and became even more influential.

In a moment of magnanimity, the emperor decreed that his consort might make an imperial visit at a prefixed date to her parents by way of fulfilling her duties of filial piety. And this usually would not happen more than once in the lifetime of an imperial consort.

To prepare for this grand occasion, the Jias spent a fortune in building a special garden for the reunion and named it Grand View Garden. It was a veritable fairyland, studded as it was with fancy pavilions, miniature mountains and artistic rockeries. It was also landscaped with bamboo or luxuriant trees that suited the atmosphere of each location and with flowers in all the blooming seasons.

In addition to the main hall for the reception of Her Highness, scattered cottages, courtyards and villas, bearing such suggestive names as "Bamboo Lodge", "Fragrant Tower", "Happy Red Court", "Alpinia Park", "Hemp-Washing Cottage", "Lotus Fragrance Anchorage", "Paddy-Sweet Cottage" and so on were built for the repose of the strollers. These were connected by winding or zigzag paths which went over the hills, by the side of rippling lakes or across bridges spanning crystal, clear streams. And more often than not, they were screened by hills or rockeries, half hidden by verdant groves or hedged in by rustic fences as befitting the various styles of architecture.

This splendid garden, dreamland of the classical landscape architect, was used only once for the reception of the imperial visitor. After that, Baoyu, his sisters, girl cousins and sisters-in-law moved in with their respective maids and servants to take up their quarters in the different houses. So the garden witnessed the heyday and the decline of the noble household, the pleasures sought by the masters, the groaning and resistance of the downtrodden slaves, the intrigues hatched by the schemers, and the tragedy of Baoyu and Daiyu.

The idea of such a grand garden has been for generations a source of inspiration for painters and plastic artists. Many a painting or horizontal scroll has been created in an attempt to give a panoramic view of the garden according to the imagination and interpretation of the artist. Others have adopted various media to portray individual scenes described in the novel.

DAIYU BURIES FALLEN FLOWERS

黛玉葬花 *(Daiyu Zang Hua)*

Daiyu, who had lost her mother and father and gone to live under the roof of relatives, met with frustrations in her love for her cousin Baoyu. In her pent-up sorrow, with no parents, no friends to unbosom her thoughts to, she developed an unsociable and self-pitying disposition. She would often sit moodily frowning or sighing over nothing at all or for no apparent reason, would give way to long spells of weeping or illness.

One late spring day, she lamented the fallen blossoms, gathered them up and buried them in a Tomb of Flowers. While she was thus engaged, Baoyu chanced upon her and overheard her singing:

As blossoms fade and fly across the sky,
Who pities the faded red, the scent that has been?

. . .

Men laugh at my folly in burying fallen flowers,
But who will bury me when dead I lie?

. . .

The day that spring takes wing and beauty fades,
Who will care for the fallen blossom or dead maid? *

This is not merely a lament from a young, broken heart, a sigh of the depressed, but also an accusation against feudal society.

The image of Daiyu carrying a basket and hoe with which to bury the fallen flowers, has been a popular theme for decorations on porcelain pieces, notably vases, as well as for paintings and works of sculpture.

* Quoted from English version of *A Dream of Red Mansions*, Foreign Languages Press, Beijing.

THE TWELVE BEAUTIES OF JINLING

十二金釵 *(Shi Er Jinchai)*

Traditional Chinese artists specialized in figure-painting like to use this subject to depict classical beauties in ancient costumes. Usually they do these in a set of twelve separate portraits.

The "Twelve Beauties" refer to the twelve leading woman characters in the novel *A Dream of Red Mansions*. Briefly, they include:

Lin Daiyu, Baoyu's sweetheart,

Xue Baochai, who was married to Baoyu by trickery,

Baoyu's sisters and female cousins,

Wives of his brother, cousin and nephew.

While these young ladies have one thing in common — beauty, they have each of them, under the masterly pen of the author Cao Xueqin, a distinctive character. There are, among them, an imperial consort who has to be queenly in attire and deportment; a sensitive and physically delicate maiden constantly consumed by sadness; the daughter of a rich family with a calculating mind under a saintly appearance; a bewitchingly attractive shrew; a young widow resigned to her fate; a teenager already disillusioned with life, and so on.

So the painter's task is not only to bring out their gorgeous or graceful dresses and their good looks but penetrate through their outward appearance to their inner being. His success provides great satisfaction to the viewer, especially one familiar with their stories. And there are many *Hong Lou Meng* fans in China!

Separate scenes involving the above characters with or without others (notably Baoyu, the young "hero") have also been made themes for paintings or sculptures, as for instance:

When Baoyu and Daiyu are reading *The Western Chamber* which as a drama of love was taboo for young people in those days (works depicting this scene are usually entitled *Du Xi Xiang* in Chinese);

When Daiyu, during one of her spells of sadness, converses with her parrot in the company of her trusted maid *(Xi Yingwu)*;

When the young people gather together over a dinner of crabs to hold a poetry contest on the subject of "chrysanthemums", in which Daiyu wins the first place *(Xiaoxiang Duo Kui)*;

When Shi Xiangyun, a tomboyish cousin of Baoyu's, falls asleep amidst flowers in the garden after she has got drunk at a party *(Xiangyun Zui Wo)*;

When Baoqin (said to be the most beautiful girl of all) goes out in a scarlet cape into the silvery world after a heavy snow in search of plum-blossoms *(Baoqin Ta Xue)*.

Traditional artists have borrowed so copiously from the novel that, it may be safe to say, when you see an old-style painting or sculpture with one or more beauties in a garden setting, there is a fair chance that it represents an episode from *A Dream of Red Mansions*.

THE TRAGEDY OF THIRD SISTER YOU

尤三姐 *(You San Jie)*

Although this story is but a ramification of the main plot of *A Dream of Red Mansions*, in itself it makes up an independent tragedy, and a stage version of it runs roughly as follows:

Jia Zhen, one of the masters of the influential Jia clan, and his cousin Jia Lian (this is the henpecked husband of none other than the pretty but formidable Wang Xifeng) were not only close kinsmen but birds of a feather in the seeking of pleasures.

Zhen was married to a wife née You, who had a widowed step-mother and two step-sisters. These young women were called simply Second Sister and Third Sister. Living in none too comfortable circumstances, the Yous became hangers-on of Jia Zhen and helped out when the latter was involved in any family exigency.

The cousins, Zhen and Lian, had designs on the two girls, who were both great beauties in spite of their strained financial straits. Second Sister was as naive and pliable as she was attractive, and soon succumbed to the advances of Jia Lian, who took her as his secondary wife on the sly and installed her in a separate house, keeping this a secret from his notoriously jealous wife. Her mother and Third Sister also moved in and shared her quarters.

In this secret marriage of his cousin, Jia Zhen had offered his share of help. He had his own motives too, that is, to have one more place where he could fool around, especially during Jia Lian's absence. One night offered such an opportunity, but his arrival at the house was followed by that of Jia Lian, who thought him interested in Third Sister and wanted to help in order to repay his past kindness.

At an improvised night drinking party, the two men got frivolous with Third Sister. Now the two sisters were poles apart in temperament. As her sister was meek and credulous, Third Sister was firm, strong-willed and skeptical, and often became satirical to the point of eccentricity. Loosening her dress, she jumped up and sat on the table, heaping jeers and taunts on the two philanderers, leaving them dumbfounded.

After that, the two ne'er-do-wells did not dare to tease or provoke her any more but decided to marry her off to the man she had been interested in all along.

She let out that, some years before, she had taken a fancy to an actor by the name of Liu Xianglian and that this would be the only man she would ever marry. But Xianglian had been out of town for some time.

On a business trip out in the province, Jia Lian met Liu Xianglian and seized the opportunity to act as go-between. Xianglian agreed to the proposed match and gave Jia Lian a pair of swords in the same sheath, an heirloom of the family, as his betrothal token for Third Sister.

Jia Lian brought home the good news as well as the swords. Third Sister was elated and shed tears of happiness. Fondling the swords at night, she was carried away by her imagination of an idyllic life spent in Xianglian's company.

But Xianglian began to have second thoughts about the engagement. Hadn't he made a hasty decision? Could the younger sister of the mistress of a Jia be the virtuous wife that he had been waiting for? He asked a couple of people who were supposed to be in the know, and all he got were evasive and uncertain replies.

He made up his mind to break off the engagement.

Calling on Jia Lian at his hide-away house, he demanded that the betrothal be cancelled and his swords returned. The argument which arose between the two was overheard by Third Sister. She came out to defend herself, protesting her innocence in spite of the circumstances she lived in. This failed to move Xianglian.

Desperate and heart-broken, Third Sister took out the pair of swords. She returned one of them to Xianglian and, with the other, she took her own life. Only then did Xianglian realize what a mistake he had made. As Third Sister lay dying in his arms, he cried out again and again, "My dear, dear wife, I've wronged you!"

Distraught and disillusioned with life, Xianglian renounced the world, cut off his hair and became a monk.

This is the story of the Peking opera entitled *Third Sister You* (in Chinese, *You San Jie*).

Incidentally, there is another play, combining the tragedy of the two sisters in one single piece entitled *Hong Lou Er You (The Two You Sisters of the Red Mansions)*. It goes on to show how the affairs of Jia Lian and simple-minded Second Sister become known to the termagant Wang Xifeng who, feigning understanding and compassion, induces her to move into the aristocratic mansion and how, maltreating and tormenting her in a subtly cruel manner, she drives her to an anguished death.

STORIES FROM THE ROMANCE OF THE THREE KINGDOMS

三國演義 *(San Guo Yanyi)*

The classical historical novel *San Guo Yanyi* (or *Romance of The Three Kingdoms*) by Luo Guanzhong (14th century) covers the period 220-280, known in Chinese history as the Three Kingdoms Period.

When the degenerating Eastern Han dynasty was shaken by the uprising of the Yellow Turbans, great confusion reigned in China with local governors and landlords fighting for control of the country. Finally three leaders emerged:

Cao Cao, leader of the Kingdom of Wei (its capital at Luoyang), occupying the Yellow River valley;

Liu Bei of the Kingdom of Shu (roughly present-day Sichuan province with Chengdu as its capital); and

Sun Quan heading the Kingdom of Wu (its capital at Wuchang and then Nanjing), which spread over the middle and lower reaches of the Changjiang (Yangtse) River.

It was a period of acute strife among the warlords, their unceasing warfare interwoven with alliance and betrayal, strategem and counter-strategem, intrigue and espionage. The novel abounds with gripping episodes, making it a rich source for dramatic material. The Peking opera, for instance, has a large repertoire based on this masterpiece. Painters and handicraft artists have also drawn liberally on this work, using it for their "suites of paintings" or for screens *(paravents)*, either painted or inlaid with stones or mother of pearls.

Here are several of the best known episodes, briefly told.

THE PEACH GARDEN PACT

桃園結義 *(Taoyuan Jie Yi)*

Towards the end of the Eastern Han, popular uprisings against the still reigning but disintegrating dynasty provided opportunities to those with great ambitions.

One day, Liu Bei standing among a group of people in front of an official notice, sighed heavily. Posted up was a call to arms. He was accosted by Zhang Fei, a total stranger, and the two struck up an acquaintance of mutual admiration. They were soon joined by Guan Yu. The three discussed the organization of a private armed force to take up their "great task" of saving the country.

Liu Bei was a descendant of the Imperial Household whose family had lost its peerage and sunk into poverty. He was now making a living on the sale of straw sandals. He was tall of stature and is said to have had extraordinarily long ears and long arms, features believed then to belong to kings or emperors.

Guan Yu, who had slain a local ruffian that bullied people and had been a fugitive for some years, was now intending to join the army. He was a man of huge frame, long beard, dark-brown face and lips of deep red. Later generations have considered him the personification of loyalty.

Zhang Fei, also tall of stature, with a head like a leopard's, large eyes, a pointed chin and a bristling moustache, was a man of fiery temperament. At this point he was a wine-seller and occasionally worked as a butcher.

The next day, in the Peach Garden of Zhang Fei's house, they took an oath of brotherhood and became bond-brothers. Then they set about recruiting people for their army. This is how the state of Shu was started by its founders.

The three lived up to their oath, remaining loving and loyal to one another throughout extraordinary tests and vicissitudes. In fact, two of them died for their common cause. This is why, over the centuries in China, the expression "peach-garden brotherhood" has come to mean the best, the most truthful friendship that people can ever hope to have.

142

DIAOCHAN PRAYS TO THE MOON

刁嬋拜月 *(Diaochan Bai Yue)*

Diaochan was a singing girl in the household of Prime Minister Wang Yun. Pretty, thoughtful and well-versed in the arts of singing and dancing, she was regarded by the Prime Minister more as a daughter than a dependant. But in her mind she was more than a singing girl and, like her master, she was constantly tormented by the deteriorating state of affairs in the country.

One late night, she was found praying alone to the moon at the Peony Pavilion in the garden. Pressed by Premier Wang, she divulged her determination to save the country from the evil clutches of Dong Zhuo even to the point of sacrificing her own life.

Now, Dong Zhuo, self-styled "Imperial Rector", was the virtual ruler of the country, keeping the Emperor as a figure-head under his thumb. He was very much hated for his greed and cruelty, even more for his undisguised ambition to usurp the throne. He would have been dealt with, had it not been for his adopted son, young General Lü Bu, noted for his military power and unparalleled prowess in the art of fighting.

Diaochan's patriotic thoughts gave Wang Yun an idea. With her consent, he initiated what he called a "double-chain strategem".

He first promised Diaochan, whom he now claimed to be his daughter, to Lü Bu in betrothal; but then he also presented her to Dong Zhuo as a concubine. When she had been carried in a sedan-chair to the mansion of the Imperial Rector, he told Lü Bu that his adoptive father was making preparations for his wedding. Lü, however, found his fiancée living in the same room with the father and there were no signs of any forthcoming ceremony for his own wedding.

At a chance encounter, Diaochan, simulating deep grief, indicated to him that she had been forced to live with the old Rector. This aroused a deep hate in Lü against Dong Zhuo. Meanwhile, Dong, having noticed the gesticulations between the two, got angry with Lü and forbade him ever to come again into his house. Thus, discord was sown between the father and his adopted son.

One day, while Dong Zhuo was having an audience with the Emperor, Lü Bu went to see Diaochan at the Phoenix Pavilion. She poured out her sadness at having to be with the old Rector and pledged her true love for him, the young general. While they were kissing, embracing and weeping, Dong burst upon the scene. He tried to kill Lü Bu with his own halberd which had been left near the pavilion, but failed.

Thus the two became deadly enemies. Finally on further instigation by Wang Yun, Lü Bu killed Dong Zhuo at court and had Diaochan for his wife.

Theatrical plays have been presented, and works of art made, of this episode under the titles: *The Double-Chain Strategem (Lian Huan Ji), The Phoenix Pavilion (Feng Yi Ting)* or *Diaochan Prays to the Moon.*

BROTHERS' REUNION AT GUCHENG

古城會 *(Gucheng Hui)*

The brotherly friendship between Liu Bei, Guan Yu and Zhang Fei, held to be exemplary though it has been, was not without an occasional misunderstanding or blemish.

At a battle in Xuzhou, the small force of the trio was put to rout by an army of superior strength under the command of Cao Cao, who had by now climbed to Dong Zhuo's position (Cf. *Diaochan Bai Yue*). Zhang Fei fled to a mountain. Liu Bei went to join Yuan Shao, another general who was also fighting Cao Cao. Guan Yu, who had to take care of the two wives of Liu Bei, was surrounded by Cao's troops and finally persuaded to surrender by a friend of his working under Cao. This he did conditionally, that is, though he might work for Cao, he would remain loyal to his sworn brother Liu Bei and, as soon as he got news about his whereabouts, he would leave to rejoin Liu. Cao had to acquiesce to his terms, hoping to win him over through generous treatment.

Cao Cao, now self-appointed Prime Minister ruling in the name of a nominal emperor in his hands, held Guan Yu in high regard, heaping honours and favours on him. In return, Guan rendered him meritorious services on the battlefield, including the felling of two great captains under Yuan Shao without knowing that his dear brother Liu Bei was taking refuge with him — a fact which nearly caused Liu his life.

News of Liu's whereabouts finally got through to Guan, and he made up his mind to leave immediately. But, true to his character, he would only go openly, as this was the way he had come. He went to the Prime Minister's palace to take leave but Cao Cao, knowing why he had come, repeatedly put off seeing him. He had to go, leaving a written notice of his departure, and a farewell message.

He set out on a long and difficult journey on his lone steed, escorting his two sisters-in-law. Travelling without proper credentials from the Prime Minister, he was forced to slay six great lieutenants of Cao's who, guarding five passes on the way, tried to stop and arrest him.

He arrived outside a mountain town called Gucheng.

Now, Gucheng was occupied by his other sworn brother Zhang Fei who, owing to a shortage of food and supplies in the mountain, had taken it by turning out the magistrate. Standing on the town wall, Zhang refused to open the gate for Guan but threatened to kill him as a traitor for having surrendered to Cao. Guan's protestations and the two ladies' entreaties were all to no avail.

At this juncture, it happened that Cai Yang, one of Cao's chief captains, who had always hated Guan Yu, arrived with a fresh levy of horsemen in pursuit of the weary Guan. In order to prove his innocence, Guan shouted to Zhang, "Brother, wait! Watch me slay the leader of these troops that I may prove myself to be no traitor!" Zhang replied, "I will help you with three rolls of the drum to see you prove your loyalty."

Before the first roll was over, Cai Yang's head was rolling on the ground.

In this way, mutual trust and friendship was restored between the brothers. The two soon joined with Liu Bei to rally their forces once more against Cao Cao.

A word should be added about Guan Yu. Because of his devotion to a prince whom he called brother, his exploits were played up and he himself was deified by later rulers and given the title of respect "Guan Gong" (Lord Guan) or even "Guan Di" (Emperor Guan). Many temples dedicated to his memory were built during various dynasties; some of them exist down to the present day.

148

THREE VISITS TO A COTTAGE

三顧草廬 *(San Gu Caolu)*

After his appointment as military prefect of Yuzhou, Liu Bei who cherished lofty ambitions, began to think of recruiting talents and scholars to help him in his cause.

There were two men whom he held in great esteem and wished to retain as his advisers, but one of them preferred to remain an idle recluse and the other, while ably carrying out his duties, unfortunately soon fell into the hands of his enemy Cao Cao. Both, however, had spoken to him highly of Zhuge Liang (an authentic historical figure, 181-234) in glowing terms of admiration. He made up his mind to enlist this man in his service as counsellor and guide.

Zhuge Liang lived in a modest cottage in the district of Nanyang by the side of the Sleeping Dragon Ridge. So, apart from his by-name Kongming, he was also known as the Master of the Sleeping Dragon. Liu Bei, accompanied by his two sworn brothers, Guan Yu and Zhang Fei, had to make three trips on horseback to visit this sage and persuade him to leave his retreat.

The first time they were there, the Master was out and they were met at the cottage door by a page, who could not tell them where his master had gone, nor when he was expected back. All they could do was to ask the lad to tell Zhuge, when he was back, that Liu Bei had called.

A few days later, on hearing that Zhuge had returned to his cottage, Liu and the two brothers made a second visit. It was a bitterly cold winter day with a fierce wind and driving snow. Zhang Fei grumblingly went along. When they arrived, however, Zhuge was out again. Liu left a note for Zhuge, expressing his admiration and saying that he would call again.

The next spring, Liu set about preparing for a third visit. He ordered lots to be cast to determine the propitious day, dieted on vegetarian food for three days and purified his body with fragrant baths (preparations for great state ceremonies in those days). The two brothers disapproved; even Guan Yu remarked that "this is showing too much deference."

At a distance from the cottage, Liu dismounted to show his respect by approaching the house on foot. At the gate, he was told that the Master was asleep. Bidding his two brothers wait outside quietly, he entered the courtyard with careful steps and waited respectfully below the steps of the house for a couple of hours until Zhuge Liang woke up to meet him.

The two held a conversation on the affairs of the country. Analysing the general situation, Zhuge pointed out to Liu how he should proceed by taking Jinzhou and Yizhou (now Sichuan province) and predicted, even before he left his cottage retreat, that the country would be divided into three states or kingdoms.

This is how Zhuge Liang started to help Liu Bei in his effort to revive the Han dynasty. Although this endeavour ended in tragic failure, yet during twenty-seven years, he helped Liu set up a well-governed kingdom in Sichuan and made six military expeditions in a bid to bring all of China under unified control. To achieve this grand mission, he said, in his own words, "I will give my all until my heart stops beating."

This pledge he lived up to in letter and spirit. The people remember his contributions and, to this day, there are still many temples in Sichuan and other provinces dedicated to his memory. He appears today as a well-appreciated character in many a Peking opera piece.

THE BATTLE OF CHIBI

赤壁之戰 *(Chibi zhi Zhan)*

This was a famous historic battle fought in the year 208, in which the far superior force of Cao Cao was badly defeated by the small combined forces of Sun Quan and Liu Bei. It is magnificently dramatised in the novel *San Guo Yanyi.* Any attempt to condense it would be doing it a great injustice; yet it would be unfair to skip it when this novel is mentioned. Hence, the following sketchy outline.

Cao Cao, having unified northern China, turned south with his great hordes, reputed to be 830,000 strong, against Sun Quan and Liu Bei.

At that time, Sun occupied the middle and lower reaches of the Changjiang (Yangtse) River with a force said to be about 60,000 strong. His followers were divided into two factions, some for resistance and the others for capitulation. Though inclined to put up a fight, he was diffident and hesitating.

Liu Bei, freshly routed by Cao and with only about 10,000 men left, had no way out unless he could combine with Sun to stop Cao's advance. His Commander-in-Chief Zhuge Liang went over to Sun's headquarters as a special envoy. There, by clever and convincing debate with the would-be capitulationists, he helped Sun make up his mind to fight.

Zhou Yu, Sun Quan's young and able Commander-in-Chief was also for war. He made a brilliant analysis of the weaknesses of Cao's apparently powerful forces: they were fatigued by a long expedition and numerous battles, they were from the North and therefore not used to warfare afloat, and most of them were newly captured enemy troops. These factors were made use of by Zhou Yu, who was good at strategem. He cleverly sowed suspicion in Cao Cao's mind and caused him to put to the sword the only two experienced commanders of his marine forces. As a ruse, Zhou had one of his own loyal lieutenants badly tortured, successfully feigning a "betrayal", which brought about Cao's destruction at the critical moment. He managed to slip a "good idea" over to

Cao to have his warships chained up, 30 to 50 in a block, ostensibly to keep them more steady for his foot soldiers but actually to make them vulnerable to attack by fire.

But none of this escaped the keen observation of the visiting envoy Zhuge Liang whom Zhou Yu looked upon as an unparallelled rival and tried to eliminate at every turn, but without success. So, there was rivalry in cooperation, intrigue in alliance. Working under such circumstances, Zhuge Liang made great contributions to the victory of the battle. On a foggy morning, he sailed with twenty boats each with bundles of straw tied to the sides, and feigned an attack on Cao Cao's warships. The latter, suspecting an ambush, forbade head-on encounter but ordered heavy shooting of arrows. By the time the fog dispersed, Zhuge had amassed more than 100,000 enemy arrows, badly needed by Zhou Yu for the final offensive. He was also knowledgeable in meteorology, it is said, and forecast easterly winds on a certain date. This was chosen as the day for an all-out attack, which was mainly by means of flaming and incendiary arrows.

On that day, the arrows carried by a favourable wind and shot from groups of small ships by Sun Quan's soldiers acting as turncoats coming over to the other side, caused a conflagration of Cao's river fleets which had been fastened into huge blocks. Not many of Cao's troops survived the disaster.

In the confusion, Zhou Yu sent men to get the head of Zhuge Liang, his provisional ally, but the astute "Master of the Sleeping Dragon" was already on a small sampan, sailing across the river to his own camp.

The Battle of Chibi was decisive. After that, Cao Cao retreated to the North, Sun Quan consolidated his hold on the lower Changjiang, and Liu Bei stabilised his occupation of Jinzhou as a base from which he later took Yizhou (Sichuan). The battle marked the real beginning of the Period of the Three Kingdoms, the tripartite partition of China which lasted for more than half a century.

STORIES FROM WATER MARGIN

水滸傳 *(Shui Hu Zhuan)*

One of the four great novels of the Ming Dynasty, *Water Margin* (also translated freely as *All Men Are Brothers*) written by Shi Nai'an (c. 1296-1370) is another almost inexhaustible source of inspiration for playwrights, artists and craftsmen.

There are a hundred and eight brave men and women in this epic novel. The majority are peasants, fishermen or other working folk, but some are small functionaries, army officers, merchants, scholars or even landowners persecuted by the higher authorities. They are all robust characters with a strong sense of justice and tremendous courage, capable of fighting to the death. Each one of them is compelled for one reason or another — corrupt officials, oppressive government or other injustices — to flee society and take refuge on Liangshan Mountain in Shandong province. They form a strong insurgent peasant army and pit themselves against the ruling dynasty. The adventures of these men are knit into an integral whole, and yet each episode can be singled out to compose an independent drama or story or to serve as the motif for artistic creation. The author's characterization is so superb that the heroes have lived in the hearts of millions generation after generation to this day, and their struggles are appraised and re-appraised again and again as history marches on. Synopses of a few well-known episodes or characters follow, but can only give a hint of the scope and power of this novel.

LU ZHISHEN WRECKS THE TEMPLE GATE

醉打山門 *(Zui Da Shanmen)*

In the novel *Water Margin*, Lu Zhishen is an indomitable warrior, hot-headed, loyal, a champion of the weak.

He first appears in the tale as a captain in the imperial army stationed in a certain prefecture in northern China. Irate over the persecution of a young woman and her father by a local gangster, who is a butcher by occupation, he kills the bully with three blows of his fist and is forced to flee from the law.

At a monastery in the Wutai Mountains, he is tonsured to become a priest without knowing anything about Buddhist doctrines or the discipline required of a monk. Within days after his ordination, he has made himself a terrible nuisance to his fellow monks by snoring through the night and by answering the calls of nature right behind the statue of Buddha in the temple hall. To climax it all, he makes a scene after drinking a misappropriated bucket of wine. The abbot, who sees the inner worth of Zhishen as a man, remonstrates with him, albeit gently. A few days' quiet ensues.

However, during his many years' service as an army officer he became accustomed to wining with big bowls and eating large chunks of meat. Before long Zhishen feels thirsty with abstinence from liquor and famished with his simple diet of vegetables.

The scene under the present title takes place when Zhishen is returning from the market place at the foot of the mountain where, pretending to be a passing priest (because people are not allowed to sell wine or meat to local priests), he fills his belly with buckets of wine and the meat of more than half a dog. Halfway up the mountain, he sits down for a rest in a pavilion. The wine rises to his head and he remembers that he has not practised his martial arts for weeks.

He tries some boxing exercises, swinging his arms up and down, back and forth, right-and left. Flinging out one arm, he strikes a pillar of the pavilion breaking it in two. Half the structure comes down.

The loud noise alarms the priests at the monastery. Having

tasted his blows before, they close the gate to keep him out. This arouses his anger and he hammers loudly on the gate with his fists, but in vain. Looking up, he sees two huge idols, the guardians of the gate, glowering down at him with raised arms. In a rage, he gets up on the pedestals and shakes the idols, flailing at their legs, and the two crumble down one after the other.

This episodes was worked up into a one-character, one-act play in Peking Opera style under the title *Zui Da Shanmen (Wrecking the Temple Gate in Drunken Wrath)*. The audience, familiar with the story, enjoyed the martial skills and fine characterization of the "hero". This piece, however, is not so much enacted nowadays as the next one, *The Wild Boar Wood*, in which Lu Zhishen also appears.

THE WILD BOAR WOOD
野猪林 *(Ye Zhu Lin)*   *or*
逼上梁山 *(Bi Shang Liangshan)*

Lu Zhishen's repeated disturbances at the Wutai Mountain monastery convinced the abbot that he should be sent away to a monastery in the capital (today's Kaifeng of Henan province). Here he was assigned to look after the vegetable garden.

Soon his physical prowess attracted a number of admirers from among the neighbourhood ne'er-do-wells who convened daily to watch him exercise or to share wine and food with him. It was at one of these gatherings that he was annoyed at the squawking of some crows that had built a nest in the willow branches. Bending the tree with his right hand and grasping the trunk with his left, he gave a jerk and up-rooted the whole tree, leaving his on-lookers dumbfounded.

One day, while he was exercising with his long, heavy iron staff, applause from outside the low garden wall reached his ears. This is how he made the acquaintance of Lin Chong, instructor of the government troops in staff and sword. The two, who had heard so much of each other, struck up a friendship immediately.

However, hardly had they expressed their mutual admiration when Lin Chong's maidservant arrived panting with news that her mistress was being molested by a group of people at the nearby temple. Lin made off with a hurried good-bye to his new-found friend.

It turned out that the man who was making passes at his wife was young lord Gao, the adopted son and sole heir of the War Minister Gao Qiu, under whom Lin Chong was but a junior officer. The Minister was as imperious as he was powerful, and the son a spoiled coxcomb whose main pleasure was seducing other men's wives and daughters.

Mutual recognition relieved Lin's wife from her impasse but Lin had to suppress his anger and the frustrated young lord Gao to take his leave. Wrathful Lu Zhishen, rushing to the scene with his friends, had to be restrained by Lin Chong.

The young ruffian, consumed by flames fanned up by the

rare but inaccessible beauty of Lin's wife, grew listless and fell into a deep languor. This alarmed his father. A scheme was offered by one of his retainers by the name of Lu Qian, who was supposed to be a good friend of Lin Chong's.

Out on the street one day Lin came across a man trying to sell a fine broad sword, which struck his fancy at once. He bought it at a reasonable price. The next day Lu Qian called on him and brought him a verbal invitation from the War Minister to come over to show him his new acquisition.

Lu guided Lin into an inner court of the Minister's palace and bade him wait while he went in to announce him to the Minister. Lin, broad sword in hand, waited for quite a while before he began to grow suspicious. Looking around, he found he was standing at the very door of the "War Hall of the White Tiger", the place where important war decisions were made and which unauthorized persons were not allowed to approach. As he was just about to move away, he was arrested by a score of soldiers and charged with the intent to assassinate the Minister with a sharp weapon found on his person.

He was tried and badly tortured but he refused to make a confession. Nor could be extricate himself. Lu Qian, the only witness who could testify in his favour, denied having ever seen him on that fateful day.

In the absence of a confession, he could not be sentenced to death as the War Minister and his son had wished. The magistrate in charge of the case was aware of his innocence but had to convict him of the crime of entering a vital military establishment without authorisation. He was branded by tattooing on the cheeks and sentenced to exile to Cangzhou, a border town near the sea.

There followed a sad parting scene between him and his beautiful wife, to whom he had been married for only three years. In view of her youth and his own uncertain future, he had prepared a bill of release for her to marry again and not to waste the prime of her life on his account. This she refused to accept, vowing that she would never become wife to another man.

At last, with his neck in an iron rack and under the escort of two guards, he had to say goodbye to his wife, father-in-law, friends and neighbours who had come to bid him farewell.

On the way, the innocent man was maltreated by his two guards. With wounds festering on his legs and feet, he made his way with great difficulty. At length they arrived at the notorious Wild Boar Wood (Ye Zhu Lin), where robberies and murders were a frequent occurrence. The guards suggested a rest but expressed their suspicions that Lin Chong would try to escape while they were asleep. To assuage their doubts, Lin agreed that they should tie him to a tree. This done, the two guards raised their clubs over him, saying that they had orders from the War Minister to kill him mid-way.

Suddenly a man burst forth from amongst the trees, roaring like thunder. In a flash, his iron staff flew out to meet the two clubs as they came down. It was Lu Zhishen, the fat priest, who had kept in close touch with all that had befallen Lin and had followed his exiled friend all the way to provide him with secret protection. In vain, he tried to persuade Lin to have the guards killed and then to take to the road. Lin preferred to serve his term in the hope that one day he might still return for a family reunion.

Thus the two brother-friends parted ways, with Lu becoming an outlaw and Lin continuing on his way to Cangzhou.

Meanwhile, back in the capital, unable to protect herself against the constant harassment of the evil young Gao, Lin's wife committed suicide.

Minister Gao and his son had no intention of leaving Lin Chong in peace at Cangzhou. They despatched Lu Qian there to get rid of him by setting fire to the government granaries which had been put in his charge. It was only when he was driven to the wall that Lin Chong in desperation rose up, killed his enemy Lu Qian with his sword, and made his way to Liangshan Mountain to join the rebels.

This story is so popular that there are at least two plays written for Peking opera alone, with basically the same plot, one under the title *Ye Zhu Lin (Wild Boar Wood)* and the other, *Bi Shang Liangshan (Driven to Revolt)*.

THE BLACK WHIRLWIND

李逵 *(Li Kui)*

Probably the most lovable character in the novel *Water Margin* is Li Kui, a true peasant — simple, blunt, generous and sincere. He is every inch a rebel, completely loyal to his fellows and so imbued with hatred for the dark forces of society that he wants to sweep them aside with the force of a whirlwind. Hence his nickname: The Black Whirlwind.

As a young hired farm hand, he is forced to flee his native place because of a murder charge. He works as a guard in the gaol of Jiangzhou, where Song Jiang (later, leader of the Liangshan forces) is imprisoned for writing a revolutionary poem. Li helps the band from Liangshan Mountain in a successful last-minute raid on the execution ground to rescue Song Jiang from imminent death.

After joining the forces in the mountain, he becomes one of the captains in the ranks of the foot soldiers and as such performs many meritorious deeds in battles with the government troops sent out on punitive expeditions against them.

A thorough-going revolutionist, he does not content himself with the elimination of a few corrupt officials but wants to "fight our way to the eastern capital and get his bloody throne", aiming his arrow directly at the Song Emperor. He is dead set against Song Jiang's line of capitulation. When at a dinner Song advocates accepting the offer of imperial amnesty, he kicks over the dining table, smashing up the bowls, cups and dishes, shouting "Amnesty! Amnesty! Amnesty be damned!" Later he beats up the envoy from the court and tears up the imperial edict.

He guards most jealously the reputation of the mountain headquarters. When he is misinformed that Song Jiang, his most respected brother leader, has had affairs with respectable women, he flares up, cuts down the flagpole and yells, "Let's disband!" But as soon as he finds out he has wronged Song, he apologizes.

In other episodes, he shows himself to be considerate and sympathetic toward the underdog and the unprivileged

Although simple, he can also be astute and humourous. His simplicity, however, is not unmixed with coarseness at times.

When he appears as a character on the traditional stage, his face is invariably painted black and white plus a touch of red and he wears a long black beard. A pair of axes are his weapons. His image in other graphic and plastic arts generally follows this pattern.

WU SONG KILLS A TIGER
武松打虎 *(Wu Song Da Hu)*

Wu Song is yet another hero of the Robin Hood type. A man of iron, of stupendous strength and courage, he goes through many ups and downs in life — avenging a murdered brother, suffering injustice and persecution, committing murders in vengeance — before he becomes thoroughly disillusioned and finally joins the band at Liangshan Mountain.

The following episode describes one of his early adventures.

Wu Song was on his way back to Yanggu county to join his elder brother after an absence from home of many long years. There was only one more mountain, the Jingyang Ridge, to cross before he would be home. Stopping at a wine shop for a meal, he noticed a sign with the warning: "Three Bowls and You Cannot Top the Ridge".

Hungry and thirsty, he ordered meat and drink. After he had eaten a hearty meal and drunk three bowls of wine, the shop-keeper would not sell him any more, explaining to the annoyed customer that although a country brew, his vintage had the taste and potency of old wine; that's why it had acquired another name: "Wine That Knocks You Down outside the Door". At the insistence of Wu Song, whose thirst had just been whetted by the first three bowls, the shop-keeper had to serve another, and then another, until the hero had finished eighteen bowls of the potent booze, six times the limit!

He picked up his bundle to continue his journey, only to be stopped by the wine seller again with the warning that in recent months a tiger had been roaming the ridge and had taken the lives of around twenty people or so. The local magistrate, he said, had stipulated that passers-by could only cross the ridge during the few hours before and after noontime, and must do so in large groups.

Wu Song took little notice of the warning and set out alone late in the afternoon, suspecting the shop-keeper of trying to get some extra business by making him spend the night at his inn. Halfway up the slope he came across an official notice confirming what the shop-keeper had said, but he was reluctant to turn back now, for it was a question of saving face.

Heady with wine, he slumped down on a rock for a rest. In a flash, a slant-eyed, white-browed tiger burst out like a howling whirlwind. Ravenous, it sprang at Wu Song, who jumped aside to dodge it. Raising the club that he carried, he aimed a blow at it but missed, swinging the club onto a tree and breaking it in two. The ensuing life-and-death struggle lasted for some time. At length he managed to grasp the tiger by the scruff of the neck and press its head down. With all his might he kicked the beast in its face and eyes. The tiger set up a terrible roaring and pawed the ground beneath its body. The scraping and scuffling wore away the dirt, and Wu Song pressed its muzzle down into the pit. The tiger began to show signs of exhaustion. Then grasping it by the neck with his left hand, Wu Song clenched his right fist into a very hammer of iron and with all the strength he could muster he struck and struck again. After some fifty to seventy blows, blood flowed out from the great beast's eyes, mouth, nose and ears. That is how Wu Song killed the tiger with his bare hands.

Quickly the news spread and the exhausted Wu Song was given a hero's welcome by the people of his native town.

STORIES FROM PILGRIMAGE TO THE WEST

西遊記 *(Xi You Ji)*

This novel by Wu Cheng'en (c. 1500-1560) drew liberally on early Buddhist legends about a famous monk. Although its characters are mostly spirits and monsters, it is full of human interest and humour. The series of adventures recounted, as gripping as they are unlikely, involve mainly:

Xuan Zang — an historically authentic monk of the seventh century who went from China to India and, after 17 years, brought back Buddhist scriptures and then translated them. In the novel, he is described as kindly and sincere, although a bit pedantic.

Monkey (Sun Wukong) — his chief disciple, the real hero of the romance, wily, irrepressible, fearless, but also kind and loyal.

Pigsy (Zhu Bajie) — his second disciple, stupid, greedy, lecherous, but at the same time simple and honest. The clown in this masterpiece, he is faithful to friends when they are in real danger.

Sandy (Sha Heshang) — his third disciple, a fallen deity. This ferocious-looking character plays merely a supporting role.

Quite a few of the adventures they go through during their westward journey (and, in the case of Monkey, before that), as described in the novel, have been adapted for stage performance with Monkey as the central figure. They are popularly known among the Chinese as "Monkey pieces". Handicraft works have also drawn their themes from the following Monkey episodes.

THE WATER-CURTAIN CAVE

水簾洞 *(Shuilian Dong)*

Many, many years ago, a "stone monkey" was born out of a rock which had been fertilised by the rays of the sun and the moon on top of the Mountain of Flowers and Fruit in the kingdom of Aolai over the seas.

He was all alone. He tried to befriend, in turn, the tigers, leopards, deer and cranes on the same mountain, but they all disregarded and shunned him.

Seeing his own reflexion one day in a stream, he realised that he was different from the other animals but looked like one of a group of monkeys whom he had seen. Venturing to join them, he was accorded a lively welcome. Only too soon, he had learned all their gambolling tricks.

They used to play around a brook in the ravine and drink from it. Where did it come from? They decided to explore. Their curiosity led them to a waterfall.

An old monkey, one of the group elders, challenged the younger ones to go through the cataract and find out what was behind it, adding, "We'll make him king, whoever goes in and comes out safely!"

Finally, it was the stone monkey who took up the challenge. Closing his eyes, he leaped through the "water curtain" and landed on an iron-plated bridge. Behind the bridge, he saw a stone stele with the inscription: "Water-Curtain Cave of the Mountain of Flowers and Fruit, Land of Bliss and Divinity".

Further on there was a real cave, furnished with tables, benches and cooking utensils all made of stone. It was large enough to accommodate about a thousand monkeys.

Delighted with his discovery, the stone monkey took back the happy news to his companions. They all went in leaping through the waterfall after his example. As promised, they made him their king.

The above anecdote marks the beginning of the popular novel *Xi You Ji*, telling us about the birth and emergence of its hero the Monkey King. Although this is not much of a story, it has been made the theme of many a piece of stone or jade sculpture. The setting of the Mountain of Flowers and Fruit or of the Water-Curtain Cave appeals to the imagination of the traditional handicraft artist as an ideal elfland, a carefree world of beauty, grace and tranquillity not to be found in the human world — in short, a fit subject for artistic creation.

MONKEY "BORROWS" A WEAPON FROM THE DRAGON KING

龍宮借寶 *(Longgong Jie Bao)*

Monkey King, having spent years on a mountain island thousands of leagues away, studying the way of Immortality under the tutelage of Patriarch Subodhi and learning seventy-two kinds of transformations, returned to the Mountain of Flowers and Fruit, where a tremendous welcome by his monkey subjects greeted him.

Because during his absence his "people" had been bullied by a monster in the neighbourhood, he decided to train the small monkeys in the arts of war. As to weapons, he removed all the arms from the royal arsenal of an earthly kingdom by magic and turned them over to his boys. He tried them out himself but found them all too light and too fragile. For want of a suitable weapon for himself, he felt desolate.

Then two monkey elders made a suggestion: Why not go to the Dragon King at the bottom of the sea? The old dragon is well-known for his various hoards of treasures.

Monkey made a magic pass, recited a spell and dived into the sea. The water opened up before him, showing him the way. But the turtle and prawn generals stopped him. They flatly refused to let him pass, or to announce his arrival to the Dragon King; that is, until they got a good dressing-down with some telling blows.

Monkey told the Dragon King that he had come to borrow a weapon from his "old neighbour". The old dragon, having heard of him, was all smiles, and quite ready to provide him with any available weapon. But a spear of three thousand pounds bent like a leather belt in Monkey's hands, and as for a halberd of seven thousand pounds, he threw it about like a wooden javelin. Monkey said that anything of this calibre would not be of much good to him.

The dumbfounded dragon pointed at a huge iron pillar rising from the bottom of the sea. Called the "magic sea-fixing needle", it had been used by the Great Yu to fix the depth of the rivers and seas after he had subdued the Great Flood (Cf. *Da Yu Zhi Shui*).

177

Monkey leapt closer to have a look, delighted with the pillar, which glowed with a strange light. "It's a pity that it's so thick," he thought. "It wouldn't do any harm if it were a little smaller." And sure enough, the pillar grew smaller until it became a cudgel of handy size for wielding against a rival, while retaining its weight of 13,500 pounds. It could even shrink to a size smaller than a sewing needle to be kept, when not needed, in Monkey's ear.

Highly pleased, Monkey played with it a while, then strode away flourishing it, without thanking the Dragon King.

Furious at the impudent monkey for having robbed him of his best treasure, the old dragon went straight up to Heaven to lodge a complaint with the Jade Emperor, supreme ruler of all.

And this leads us to the next episode about how Monkey created havoc in Heaven.

HAVOC IN HEAVEN

大鬧天宮 *(Da Nao Tiangong)*

The Jade Emperor, on hearing the Dragon King's complaint, was about to order the Heavenly King Li Jing* to arrest the unruly Monkey, when old angel Taibai, Spirit of the Planet Venus, advised His Majesty to use pacifying rather than punitive methods in dealing with this upstart. The Emperor gave this mission to Taibai.

Taibai did his job well. He persuaded Monkey to come to Heaven and take up the post of *Bimawen*. This, he was assured, was a High Office and on his premises, which were the Imperial Stables, he would be under nobody else. Monkey did not question much but rather enjoyed himself at the beginning, galloping on the heavenly horses.

The Jade Emperor ordered the Deity of Horses to look in on how things were going. Monkey got furious when he found out that he was expected to be subserviently respectful to this overbearing petty official and that his own job was nothing better than that of head-groom of the divine horses. He made a scene and absconded back to the Mountain of Flowers and Fruit.

To show his defiance of the Hierarchy of the Upper Realms, he bestowed on himself the high-sounding title "Great Saint, Equal of Heaven" and hoisted a banner bearing the words in bold letters.

All this served to bring down a punitive expeditionary force from Heaven headed by the aforesaid Li Jing. In trials of strength and of supernatural powers, however, Monkey emerged victorious. The expedition failed to subjugate him.

Once again, it was the cunning and smiling Taibai who came to the Mountain of Flowers and Fruit, this time to bring him imperial sanction of his title as "Great Saint" and to invite him back again to assume an official post. Monkey

---

* This is Nezha's father after he had been deified; he is usually shown holding a miniature pagoda as his magic weapon. See *Nezha Nao Hai*.

refused at first but, less experienced in the ways of the world than the old Planet Spirit, he allowed himself to be cajoled for the second time into going along.

He was put in charge of the Western Queen Mother's Peach Garden (see article under *Xi Wangmu*). And shortly after he entered on his duties, the peaches ripened. This happens only once every three thousand years, and the Queen Mother was about to hold her three-thousand-yearly Peach Banquet. When fairy maidens were sent to pick the peaches for this grand occasion, they found nothing but snapped stalks on many of the trees. Wondering about this, they woke up Monkey who, having regaled himself with the divine fruit of Immortality and changed himself by magic into a tiny form, was sleeping on a big peach.

Monkey became angry again when he heard from the girls that he was not invited to the banquet. Despite his impressive title for which he had been accorded imperial approval, he meant nothing to high society in Heaven.

He goes to the banquet hall anyway, where some waiters and servants are preparing the wine and the refreshments. By magic he puts them all to sleep and helps himself to the drinks and viands. When he has had too much, he puts all the leftovers into a magic bag for his monkey subjects back at home. In his drunkenness, he has reduced the banquet hall to a shambles.

Anticipating trouble, he wants to sneak home, but still under the influence of alcohol, he wanders by mistake into the Palace of Laozi, Grand Alchemist and Supreme Patriarch of Taoism. Finding nobody in the laboratory, he picks up a big gourd full of elixir pills, which took the old Patriarch hundreds of years to prepare, and swallows them all.

At the Mountain of Flowers and Fruit, the monkeys were delighted to see their king back. And there was great celebration and feasting.

Before the festivities were over, however, an army of

celestial warriors descended in great strength on a second punitive expedition, and laid siege to the Water-Curtain Cave.

There followed a fierce and prolonged contest of magical powers as well as physical prowess, with Monkey battling, one after another, the Kings of the Four Quarters, the pagoda-wielding Li Jing, his son Nezha, and the God Erlang, a nephew of the Jade Emperor's. It was during a protracted fight against the latter that Monkey was struck by the Diamond Snare cast by Laozi from the flank and, at the same time, bitten on the calves by the malicious Sky Hound of Erlang. Poor Monkey! Bedraggled, he was taken captive and tied to a stake on the execution block.

But no manner of execution ordered by the Emperor, neither swords nor spears, neither shooting with arrows nor burning with sacred fire, had any effect on him at all, because he had been born out of stone and had just been made more invulnerable by the peaches of Immortality, the wines of Heaven and the Elixir of Long Life.

At the suggestion of Laozi, he was put into the Crucible of the Eight Diagrams to be smelted with alchemic fire. At the end of the required forty-nine days, as the lid was taken off, Monkey, further tempered and steeled by the sacred fire, leapt out of the crucible, to the great horror of the Taoist Patriarch.

He got safely back to the Mountain of Flowers and Fruit, and there was great jubilation in his monkey kingdom.

Later on, in the novel *Xi You Ji (Pilgrimage to the West)*, Monkey becomes a disciple of the Buddhist monk Xuan Zang and accompanies him on a pilgrimage to the West (India) in search of the original Buddhist sutras. On the way, he protects his master from many monsters and spirits.

MONKEY SUBDUES THE DEMON

三打白骨精 *(San Da Baigujing)*

The monk Xuan Zang (also known as Tripitaka or Monk of Tang) is on the way to India to seek the Buddhist scriptures, accompanied by his three disciples, Sun Wukong (Monkey), Zhu Bajie (Pigsy) and Sha Heshang (Sandy). They come to a big mountain as dusk is falling. The place is marked by precipices reaching high into the skies and permeated by a miasmal mist. Monkey warns his companions to be on their guard, as he thinks there may be monsters in the neighbourhood.

Pigsy laughs at Monkey for being over-scrupulous and complains that he has already an unbearable hunger. Monkey offers to go scouting round to see if there is anything suspicious on this uninhabited mountain and also if he can find any wild fruit to bring back for them to eat. Before going away, he draws a big circle on the ground with his magic weapon, the gold-clasped cudgel, and asks his master and two fellow disciples to remain inside, no matter what happens, for their own safety.

Soon after Monkey is gone, a young country girl with a basket of bread on her arm comes along, chanting Buddha's name. Catching the appetizing smell of the newly-steamed bread, Pigsy jumps out of the circle, only to scare the girl off with his ugly features. She denounces him as a monster.

Introducing herself as the daughter of a family of Buddha's worshippers, she says that she is sent by her parents to make offerings at a nearby temple.

Pigsy begins to urge his master to go to the temple to get some food, but Sandy insists that they should wait till Monkey is back. While Tripitaka is hesitating, Monkey comes down from a shred of cloud and immediately recognizes the country lass as a demon which has formed itself from a heap of white bones. With a swing of his gold cudgel, he "kills" the girl, to the great consternation of his master Xuan Zang.

But he soon finds that the body which fell to the ground is but a disguise assumed by the White-Bone Demon, while

184

the evil spirit herself (for it usually takes the form of an elegantly-dressed woman warrior) has fled into the air. With a leap, Monkey goes after her in hot pursuit.

The demon turns back to the spot in other forms — first as the mother and then as the father of the country girl, looking for their missing daughter, then lamenting to Tripitaka over her sad fate and complaining bitterly of the cruelty with which she was slain. On both occasions, Monkey returning in time to protect his master, sees through the ruse, but like the first time, he kills only the disguise while the real demon flees.

The deluded monk gets more and more angry with his loyal disciple over the apparent slaying of all three members of a family. He is egged on by the nagging remarks of Pigsy, who is unhappy about having missed the company of a nice girl as well as the opportunity of getting a badly-needed bite to eat. In the end, in spite of Sandy's defence of Monkey, Tripitaka disowns him and banishes him back to the Mountain of Flowers and Fruit, his birthplace.

The rest of the party moves on and soon comes to an impressive Buddhist temple. No sooner have they come in and prostrated themselves before the statues than they hear the laughter of the White-Bone Demon and her followers. It turns out that the temple and its fixings are but phantasms she has conjured up to lure Tripitaka in. The brief struggle that follows ends in the capture of the monk and Sandy, while Pigsy, knowing his own limitations, flees to the Mountain of Flowers and Fruit to seek Monkey's help.

Monkey turns a cold shoulder to all entreaties for aid, but as soon as the distraught Pigsy leaves, he makes for the trouble spot in one somersault.

Pigsy, in a last desperate attempt to save his master, is also seized by the monsters.

The White-Bone Demon and her entourage are making preparations to feast on Tripitaka, whose flesh is believed to give the eaters immortality. But they have to wait for the arrival of the Demon's mother, who is to share the delicacy.

In the meantime, the old matron, carried in a sedan-chair by a group of goblins, is spotted by Monkey from the sky. He demolishes them all and changes himself into a replica of the mother demon and, with a few hairs plucked from his coat, creates an identical group of sedan-carriers.

The sham mother demon is welcomed to the cave with fanfare. She is highly delighted with her daughter's exploit and, in front of the victims, asks her how she has managed to outwit a group with such a clever Monkey in it.

Whereupon the daughter relates with pride how she sowed discord between Tripitaka and his chief disciple Monkey by appearing, in succession, as three members of a family and pretending to be killed. While relating her story, she transforms herself once again into the country girl, then her mother and finally her father. Tripitaka is dumbfounded.

The "mother demon" asks Tripitaka where his first disciple is. He sighs, "Ah, how I have wronged him!"

On hearing this confession, Monkey is so moved that he cannot continue with the theatre. Emerging as his true self, he starts a free-for-all, in which arms clash, magic weapons are conjured up and heads set rolling. In the end, the White-Bone Demon is burnt into its original shape, a heap of white bones, by fire blown out of Monkey's mouth.

The party resumes its journey to the West.

STORIES FROM THE YANG FAMILY OF GENERALS

楊家將 *(Yang Jia Jiang)*

This is the title of a Ming dynasty classical novel. Although it has never occupied an important place in the history of Chinese literature, its stories have become immensely popular through the ages, thanks to the market-place storytellers and opera writers who have drawn heavily on this source. Scenes from this novel are also found in many other forms of popular art.

The stories are based on the exploits of an historical figure Yang Ye (?-986 A.D.) and his nine children (seven boys and two daughters, nearly all distinguished warriors), who helped the Northern Song emperors during the early years of the dynasty to defend the country against the Qidan (Khitan) and the Xixia, marauders from the north and the northwest.

Before giving the synopses of a couple of the dramatic events, it would be advisable to introduce briefly the characters that appear most often in them.

Lady She, the old Dowager — After the death in action of her husband Yang Ye, founder of the famous house, she remained for many years the grand matriarch of the clan, outliving all of her children.

Yang Yanzhao — The sixth son, he was the only male of the second generation to survive his brothers, most of whom laid down their lives fighting. He served on several occasions as commander of the border garrison or marshal of an expeditionary force.

Yang Zongbao — Son of Yanzhao and the only child of the third generation, he married Mu Guiying and, like his father, died a marshal.

Mu Guiying — A heroine marked both for her intelligence and her courage. During the chaotic times prior to and following the founding of the Song empire, she was at the head of a local force organized for self-defence at her native place Mukezhai. Resisting unification of the country by the Song emperor, Guiying finds herself locked in battle with Zongbao, whom she captures alive by ambush. Impressed by his talents

188

and handsome looks, she offers herself as his bride and pledges to go over to the Song. She is the principal character in several of the *Yang Jia Jiang* stories and plays, in which the actress playing her part is expected to shine not only in singing and acting but also in fighting.

Yang Wenguang — Son of Zongbao and Guiying, he was the only boy of the fourth generation, also a fighter.

Yang Hong — The old faithful majordomo of the family, he lived and worked till over a hundred years old, like his mistress the Lady Dowager.

The Eighth Prince — An imperial prince with special powers, he usually appears on the stage as an elderly man in royal attire. He was also the brother of Yang Yanzhao's wife.

Kou Zhun — The astute elderly prime minister. He and the prince were friends of the Yang family.

Meng Liang and **Jiao Zan** — Loyal, bold chief lieutenants of Marshal Yang Yanzhao. Years later, their sons, Meng and Jiao junior, served as chief lieutenants to Yanzhao's son Zongbao, when the latter was appointed commander.

THE MARSHAL SENTENCES HIS OWN SON TO DEATH

轅門斬子 *(Yuan Men Zhan Zi)*

When Mu Guiying took a fancy to her captive Yang Zong-bao and "proposed" to him, the young general, though far from indifferent to her beauty, refused to marry the woman leader of a rebel force. When Guiying promised to join the Song army against the invading Khitan, he agreed, and they were married.

Released after the wedding, Zongbao went back to head-quarters to report to his father Yang Yanzhao, marshal of the government mission to drive out the Khitan invaders. Angered by his son's breach of discipline in marrying an adversary, the marshal sentenced him, his only son, to death and had him tied up outside the main gate for execution.

When Marshal Yang turned a deaf ear to the pleadings of his two lieutenants, Meng Liang and Jiao Zan, they hurried to enlist the help of the Eighth Imperial Prince and the Lady Dowager She, who happened to be at the front. In spite of the weight they usually carried with Yanzhao — one as the marshal's own beloved mother and the other as his brother-in-law and a venerable prince — their intervention in Zongbao's behalf was also of no avail. The argument that executing Zongbao would mean depriving the Yangs of their only male descendant fell on deaf ears too.

At this juncture, an unexpected visitor was announced. The name frightened the marshal out of his wits, for he had suffered an ignoble defeat at her hands. It was Mu Guiying who was calling in full regalia on a lone steed. Assuming an air of calmness, he declined to recognize her as his daughter-in-law until she threatened him with drawn sword. She quickly followed up with her "dragon-taming staff", a magic weapon indispensable in breaking up the Khitan's bewitched troop formation which had cost the Song many lives.

The marshal pardoned his son. And Guiying pledged allegiance to the throne and became henceforth an important and charming member of the family as well as a great lady general of the Song dynasty.

WOMAN WARRIORS OF
THE YANG FAMILY

楊門女將 *(Yang Men Nü Jiang)*

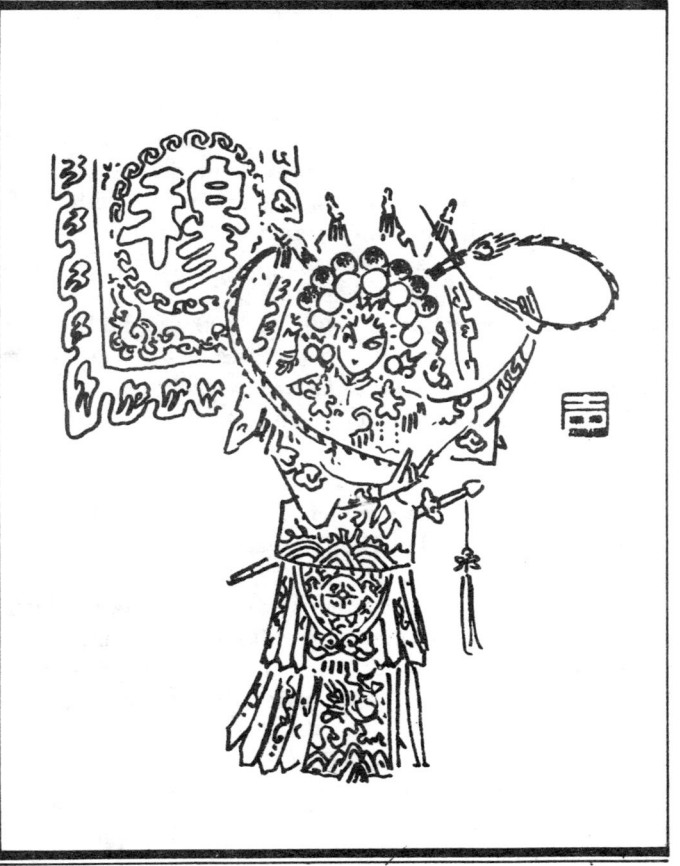

Busy preparations are being made in the mansion of the Yangs to celebrate a big occasion, the 50th birthday of Marshal Yang Zongbao, who is absent at the front engaged in fighting against Xixia*. Princess Chai (the marshal's mother, namely, widow of Yang Yanzhao) and Mu Guiying (his wife, also turning 50 herself) are in high spirits, overseeing the decoration of the hall set for the birthday banquet.

Yang Hong, the centenarian butler, announces two unexpected visitors just back from the battle front: Meng and Jiao the juniors who are the chief lieutenants of the commanding marshal. Struck by the plain clothing of the two officers, the ladies receive from them the sad report that Zongbao has died at the front from the wound of a poisonous arrow shot by the enemy. Weeping with grief, the mother and daughter-in-law admonish the two men to keep the shocking news from the Lady Dowager but to attend the banquet as if nothing has happened.

During the celebration, however, the 100-year old Dowager becomes suspicious about the evasiveness of the two officers and the unusual behaviour of Guiying. Under her persistent questioning, the sad truth comes out. And immediately, the festivities become clouded with a funereal atmosphere.

The family of the Yangs, with the exception of Wenguang, the only son of Zongbao, are left a family of twelve widows of three generations. The Lady Dowager leads them in taking an oath of vengeance.

The emperor is upset by the irreparable loss of a veteran commander and does not know whom to appoint in his place. A controversy arises between the octogenarian Prime Minister Kou Zhun, who is for giving the command over to

---

* Xixia or Western Xia, a separate rival kingdom (1038-1227) composed of various nationalities and covering parts of present-day Ningxia, Shaanxi and Gansu in China's northwest, often at war with the Song, the Liao (Khitan) and later the Jin (Golden Tartars) until wiped out by the Mongols.

the women of the Yang family, and the Deputy Prime Minister Wang, who is skeptical about the fighting qualities of women.

A personal visit of condolence to the Yang mansion by the emperor, accompanied by his two chief ministers, and a talk with the Dowager, decide the issue. In answer to the Deputy Premier Wang's remark that the widows, in their zeal to fight the enemy, are putting their personal hatred above the interests of the state, the old lady recounts the deaths, all in the battlefield, of her husband, her sons and sons-in-law, and now her grandson. If it is for personal vengeance, she concludes, they can never settle their scores with the enemy, for there are far too many. The emperor agrees that the Lady Dowager, at the age of 100, take command of the expedition.

Hence, this dramatic piece is also entitled *Twelve Widows on a Western Expedition (Shi Er Guafu Zheng Xi)*.

Newly-widowed Mu Guiying is appointed commander of the vanguard force and she brings along her young son Wenguang.

The enemy, recovering from the first blow delivered by the woman warriors, become firmly entrenched in a camp located on a steep mountainside, hoping to wear out the Song forces, which are handicapped by an over-extended supply route.

Guiying finds out that her late husband met his death when out with a small party of men in a bottle-necked valley on the other side of the mountain and deduces from this that he intended to subdue the foe in a surprise attack from behind. She suggests to the Lady Dowager that they follow up the late marshal's plan.

This is put into execution with Guiying herself leading the risky surprise party. The enemy headquarters is raided at dawn, with the Song expeditionary forces led by the woman warriors scoring a resounding victory.

PRONUNCIATION OF ROMANIZED CHINESE NAMES

Assuming that you are not studying Chinese seriously as a second language, you would not be far off if you simply pronounced the Romanized Chinese names and words generally as if they were English. Only bear in mind the following exceptions:

A. Every vowel should be sounded. There is nothing like a silent *e* at the end of a word or a syllable.

B. The following consonants represent special sounds in Chinese, different from what they might stand for in English:

    1) *c* sounds like *ts* in *cats*.

    2) *g* (as an initial) is invariably pronounced like *g* in *go* (never like *j*).

    3) *q* sounds roughly like *ch* in *ch*eese.

    4) *r* (as an initial consonant) sounds like *s* in *leisure*.

    5) *x* represents a sound which has no equivalent in English. Formerly written as *sh*, it is a consonant sound somewhere between *s* in "sea" and *sh* in "she".

    6) *zh* stands for the sound of *j* as in *j*ug.

C. The following vowel signs have their peculiarities in Chinese pronunciation, to wit:

    1) *a* normally sounds like "ah".

    2) *e*, when not in a diphthong, sounds like *er* in English (not American) "her".

    3) *i* normally sounds roughly like *i* in "s*i*t", but after the initials *c, ch, j, q, r, s, x, z,* or *zh*, it serves only to make the preceding initial consonant very much sounded without changing the position of any part of the speech organ.

    4) *u* normally sounds more or less like *oo* in "b*oo*k" but when placed after the initials *j, q, x* or *y* or when written as *ü*, it sounds like *u* in the French "r*u*e".

If you are already used to the Wade system of spelling, you may also find the names, etc. you are looking for spelt in this method in the index on the following pages, if they are covered by this book.

INDEX

199

Kuan Yü, cf. Guan Yu
Kuifei Ch'u Yü, cf. *Guifei Chu Yu*
Kuifei Tsui Chiu, cf. *Guifei Zui Jiu*
Kun, cf. Gun
Kung Kung, cf. Gonggong
Kuo Mo-jo, cf. Guo Muoro

201

206